BLUEBIRDS USED TO CROON IN THE CHOIR

BLUEBIRDS USED TO CROON IN THE CHOIR
JOE MENO

NORTHWESTERN
UNIVERSITY
PRESS
EVANSTON, ILLINOIS

TRIQUARTERLY
BOOKS

TriQuarterly Books
Northwestern University Press
www.nupress.northwestern.edu

Printed in the United States of America

10   9   8   7   6   5   4   3   2   1

ISBN 0-8101-5167-7

Grateful acknowledgment is made to the following publications, where these stories first appeared: *Bridge* ("Mr. Song"); *Chicago Tribune* ("Midway"); *Gulf Coast* ("A Trip to Greek Mythology Camp"); *Hair Trigger* ("In the Arms of Someone You Love"); *Kiss Machine* ("How to Say Good Night"); *Mid-American Review* ("Our Neck of the Woods"); *Other Voices* ("Happiness Will Be Yours"); *Pigeon* ("Hold On to Your Hat"); and *The 2nd Hand* ("Astronaut of the Year," "A Strange Episode of *Aqua Voyage,*" and "Tijuana Women").

Library of Congress Cataloging-in-Publication Data

Meno, Joe.
    Bluebirds used to croon in the choir / Joe Meno.
      p. cm.
    ISBN 0-8101-5167-7 (alk. paper)
    1. United States—Social life and customs—Fiction. I. Title.
PS3563.E53B58 2005
813'.54—dc22

                         2005019766

FOR KOREN, TO WOO YOU

With thanks to Dan Sinker, Johnny Temple, Jon Resh, Susan Betz, Johanna Ingalls, Todd Dills, Jenny Bent, Jim Munroe, Todd Taylor, Sean Carswell, Jim Vickery, Mickey Hess, Megan Stielstra, Meghan Galbraith, Mark Zambo, Todd and Ashley Baxter, Jake Silker, Sheryl Johnston, Michelle Kroes, the *Chicago Tribune,* the *Chicago Reader,* the *Chicago Sun-Times,* and the Columbia College Chicago Fiction Writing Department

CONTENTS

BLUEBIRDS USED TO CROON IN THE CHOIR

THE USE OF MEDICINE

It was the summer that we, of our own guts, decided to become anesthesiologists. It was the summer that my twin sister and I went about capturing the smallest animals we could find and placing them in dirty green glass jars that smelled of brine. Somehow we discovered our father's medical tools hidden inside a suitcase in the attic of our garage. The case was coated in gray dust and had the fingerprints of ghosts along every hinge. When we unclasped the rusty latch, a sepia picture of our parents as children in love slipped out. There was my father in a bow tie and my mother in a starchy gown with a string of pearls that smiled along her neck like a second mouth. We put the photograph back in the case, held our hands over our lips, and went about pawing through the strange silver instruments, looking for something to take the bleary boredom out of the end of a summer that was meant to be intensely recuperative.

The house was to be completely silent at all times. Our mother direly needed rest and quiet. We were told this time and time again even though my sister and I had given up talking completely, relying instead on elaborate hand signs. We were making our own language at the time, one without any words. It was a kind of code where you would spread your fingers to resemble a sparrow to indicate that you wanted to go outside, but then by making the same gesture over your eyes, you might signal that you were sad or angry or very tired. The language was so imperfect that it was deeply beautiful. Each sign meant three things at least, and the other's response was so inaccurate that it gave both of us the sense we were psychic, because it was impossible that the signs we shared could not be right. We were concerned with discussing only one thing, so every expression our hands made told the same story over and over again, each motion, each sign. On the first day of summer, my mother's birthday, our father had hung himself in the cellar, and the sound of that act was something none of us could get out of our minds.

Once we found the medical bag, however, the summer began to turn on its end for the better. Beyond the silvery scalpels and slender forceps and blunt tweezers, which our father had sometimes used to remove splinters from our fingers, we found something extraordinary: a hypodermic needle and a small vial of belladonna, marked DANGER! *PELIGROSO!* SEDATIVE.

It was not long before we began to make use of the stuff.

We decided to try it out on an insect, because it seemed pretty clear that insects were intended for this sort of experiment; if something went wrong and the patient were to die, it seemed very unlikely the creature would suffer much or be missed by family or friends after inexcusably expiring. Also, for the most part, insects were indubitably hard and not tender soft. Scientifically, it seemed the luxury of pain and the accompanying recipient of pain, the soul, which we had been forced to recognize in Sunday school, resided within things that were soft. So my sister argued at least—Isabella being born three full minutes before me. An expeditious and more complete knowledge would always be her destiny.

We sedated things in this order, with varying success: crickets, horseflies, bumblebees, wood bees, caterpillars, tiger moths, grasshoppers, stick bugs, box elder bugs, stag beetles, and, finally, a single pill bug, which rolled up inside itself to rest and somehow never awoke again. In this first series of experiments, we decided a lower dosage was preferable to a higher one; it seemed a high dose always ended with the patient becoming quite stiff and then spilling out its milky innards in a frenetic paroxysm of death. Most of the patients who were revived, however, simply hopped or flew or buzzed away without any noticeable kind of side effect—except for the only victim I was allowed to inoculate, a big golden wood bee. I accidentally punctured the wing handling the hypodermic carelessly, and the poor fellow ended up flying in circles around our heads before wearing himself to a paralytic state and eventual submission to an exhaustive death. For the most part, I was the recorder of the experiments: hypothesis, tools used, process, results, conclusion. After the first few experiments, I simply wrote "See experiment 1" if the patient expired or "See experiment 5" if the patient managed to survive.

What really happened next was that I began to get bored watching my older sister have all the fun. As always, Isabella was bossy, and after the mauling of the wood bee, I was not allowed access to any of the instruments. So on my own, I decided to change the nature of the experiments. Instead of simply sedating the animals, I thought it would be much better to sedate them for a purpose, and the purpose I selected was, without a doubt, fantastic.

We would dress the animals up while they were asleep.

It was simple enough, really. My twin sister had a number of small doll outfits, cut perfectly to size for small four-legged creatures like frogs, toads, salamanders, and field mice. We spent half the day trapping our quarry with leftovers from the lunch that the boil-necked nurse prepared for our mother, who was making no marked improvement, and the second half was devoted to sedation and fitting of clothing.

For the most part, the animals did not seem to mind. My twin had become so adept that rarely was there a fatality, and in the small number of cases where the patient died, a fawn-colored bunny, for example, it seemed all the more fitting that the deceased be dressed in small white bloomers and a velvety blue jumper. As my sister's skill with the hypodermic improved, I, too, found myself able to match almost any animal to a corresponding outfit with a certain degree of alacrity. I could tie a row of miniature pink bows along any woodland creature's tail, coordinate miniature hoods and skirts without fail, and even find funereal slippers of a silver hue for a blind shrew, which my sister oversedated, thinking it was a mole with a much more durable constitution.

The animals, when they awoke, would at first fuss about in their garments, but slowly, slowly, my twin and I could see the patients enjoying themselves, prancing about and admiring their new couture before disappearing back into the high prairie grass and then the woods. I often imagined a small child—or, even better, a hunter of some kind—stumbling upon our beauties as they savaged about, spotting a pink lace nightgown on a dove white rabbit or a turtle with ribbons along its appendages and a shell painted cornflower blue. I guess to someone the experiment might, at this turn, seem unnecessary and cruel. I would bid that someone to take hold of a magnifying glass and study the dusky apparatus of his own youth. Someone might argue that what we did lacked any meaning or motive, that we were simply terrorizing these innocent animals, but, in fact, it was after several successful sedations, and their subsequent costumings, that we stumbled upon our true purpose.

(I would like to take credit for the notion, but, truly, it was my twin sister who got the idea for the parade.)

Having properly acquainted herself with the medical way, my sister, Isabella, after long hours of watching our mother alternating between crying and sipping lentil broth at her bedroom window, a motion that seemed quite heartrending and replete with mucus, came to a diagnosis. Our mother had suffered a horrible shock, almost like a victim of electrocution. She found our father hanged in the cellar, but not only that, it was on her birthday. It seemed scientific to believe a shock of a most equal and opposite magnitude would have a definite curative effect. Scientifically, we decided a parade of costumed animals would do the trick.

We spent the next three days trapping animals of all kinds. We were running out of sedative very quickly, so if the therapy was to take place, it would have to be soon. The animals we selected were a garter snake, which I decorated with several bells and ribbons; three baby rabbits, which Isabella dressed in matching gold skirts; several frogs, which looked dapper in fitted black pants and accompanying jackets; and a salamander, who wore gloves. As it was, there was just enough sedative for all the animals. Isabella, being very cautious not to provoke an overdose, emptied the contents of the vial as gently as a trained nurse. Then I went to work. Soon enough, all the animals had been sedated and then dressed, and we could hear our mother's teakettle whistling from inside the kitchen, which meant she would be waking soon.

We pushed the small red wagon out in front of our mother's bedroom window and gingerly arranged the ornamented animals in a small ellipse on the soft side lawn. When all the slumbering participants were in place, my twin and I began to shout loudly.

My mother came to the window, panicked, holding both hands over her chest. She stared at us for signs of injury, and when she was sure we were all right, she looked down at the still-stagnant queue sleeping quietly at our feet. Our mother stood transfixed, somewhere on the brink of dreamlike wonder and horror, and in that moment it seemed the experiment could have gone either way.

But something had gone wrong. Our patients were not waking.

My mother stood there with her hands over her heart, seeing the delicate shambles, the massacre in pink and white bows, and then she turned away.

It was at that moment my sister realized the mistake. The sedative at the bottom of the vial had been more powerful; somehow it had not been diluted by light and movement and time. The usual dosage had been fatal for all the patients involved, and the parade had turned into an execution by default.

Isabella shook her head, crying into the corner of her own arm, whimpering very gently and hiding her face.

"What? What's wrong?" I asked, not remembering the timbre of my own voice. I was getting angry and anxious seeing her lose her control and demeanor like that because I still did not understand what exactly had happened.

"Matthew," she whispered. "We . . . we . . . we made a mistake."

"What? What is it?" Before she spoke, I suddenly imagined my father hanging in the cellar again, the rope encircling his neck, his eyes tightly closed, the thoughts of regret, the resolve that had driven him to his end weighing heavy in his head. What had he been thinking? What would he have said? In that instant I understood what he had discovered. The sound of my sister's voice, which had become so unfamiliar, was now the sound of the realization he had made echoing in my brain: Medicine never cures the heartaches.

OUR NECK OF THE WOODS

1

What is Pilgrimtown now? Pilgrimtown is gone. Pilgrimtown is nothing. Gone is Rural Route X. Gone are the mini-mall and Sharkey's combination auto parts warehouse, scuba dive outlet, and adult bookstore. Gone is St. Dolores's glow-in-the-dark cemetery. And gone, gone is the Mold-o-Form plastics factory, the true town, the town within the town, the nation's sole producer of commemorative plates, green pee-pee dolls, and life-size deer-shaped lawn decorations—the same factory where the boys and girls of Pilgrimtown lost limbs, lost lives, and, worse still, lost time and in the end were given a choice for their severance: a set of President Eisenhower collectible plates or a family of deer to display on their front lawns in quiet exchange for the hours and days and years of their faded existence. Gone is the dream of the new mobile home. Gone is the notion of inground plumbing. Gone are the fantasies of new wigs, liposuction, divorce, a yellow Corvette. Gone is the world of what we knew of just about everything.

If Pilgrimtown had an anatomy, if it is possible for a Pennsylvania town to have organs the way men and women have eyes and ears and brains, then the Mold-o-Form factory was its hands, its sick, embittered heart, and its terrible gnashing teeth. There were hundreds of vats, hundreds of sheet presses, and hundreds of assembly lines within the plant. All had been coordinated to move perfectly in time, much like the circulatory system of a madman, but the sheer noise of it all and the accompanying green vapor that seemed to rise with each compression of its mechanical heart forced people in Pilgrimtown to speak very, very quickly in between monstrous beats and leaks of strange glowing steam: "Yes-sir-I-would-be-happy-to-work-overtime-thank-you-sir."

Built in 1943 as a producer of plastics for military use, the plant came under commercial ownership after the war and secured for itself a safe monopoly in the unsure world of American plastic novelties. Mold-o-Form's best seller to date? "Deer Decoration 3: Fawn Gently Sipping at Brook." The popularity of that particular decoration was somewhat unsettling. In row after row of big white houses in every suburb of every city in the world stood the deer nick-named Fannie the Fawn by Mold-o-Form's industrious salesmen. The deer was ubiquitous, appearing in such numbers as to be totally terrifying: head lowered over slender legs, spry white tail rising skyward, drinking at some imaginary river no one could see. Certainly someone, some salesman, had to ask why. What was wrong in all our hearts? What were we wishing for in bed, at night, almost asleep? What missing part of our world drove us to purchase this plastic animal, put it in the backseat of our station wagons, and display it proudly in front of our homes for all our neighbors to see? What hated part of ourselves were we trying to compensate for? We don't know—we still don't really know—the answer to these questions.

Because it all ended like this: Bob Underwood was foreman of Mold-o-Form line 60, which produced Fannie the Fawn. A likable guy in his forties with a wife and two kids, he was Pilgrimtown's high school junior varsity wrestling coach and had a blond crew cut, a medium gut, and arms large enough to carry four life-size plastic deer at a time. He was a good foreman. Suspicious of the two-hour line position change, which had workers switch positions to keep from losing their minds, he asked everyone what their best spot on the assembly line was and allowed them to work that for the eight hours straight, raising quality, worker morale, and productivity. Line 60 also had the fewest flash fires, which were short, powerful explosions caused by conveyer belt friction against the newly formed and still-warm plastic deer bodies, usually the result of chit-chat or daydreaming.

In secret, late at night, sometimes after the wife and kids had gone to bed, Bob, at the kitchen table, would sketch ideas for new lawn decorations: a trio of scampering raccoons, a sharp-beaked blue-striped heron spearing a salmon, and his own personal favorite, a doe nursing two brown-eyed fawns. He showed no one these sketches, not even his wife. Instead, he kept them hidden in a tiny notebook that he carried in his back pocket at all times, hopeful that one day some administrator, some hotshot like Mr. Bruin, would ask him what he thought of something and Bob would smile, pause, and then take out the drawings and really show them what he could do.

A girl was hired for line 60 one morning, a foreign girl named Elsa with dark eyes and fluffy brown hair, a girl new to both the town and the country. It was said she was from somewhere in Eastern Europe and had worked in Mold-o-Form factory 38 before it had exploded and incinerated most of her town in a single iridescent blast of green plastic flame. As compensation, the twelve remaining survivors of the plant disaster were given jobs and relocated to the States with permanent work visas good only at the Pilgrimtown factory. The foreign girl, Elsa, had a small face and wide eyes and a mouth that seemed incapable of admitting pleasure. It was the look all of them had. The girl was very slight, very tiny, and because of her size, Elsa was immediately put in the third position on the assembly line. It was her job to paint the left eye of the lifeless deer as they passed, each socket receiving a single circular dab of glossy black, while another worker, some nonunion worker, someone like Mary Edwards, who was only part-time anyway, would, at the same time, stand across the great black conveyer belt and paint the right eye. Position 3 was directly across from position 4, and these were the only jobs on the line where there was the opportunity to look at someone else's face at all during the eight-hour shift. It was a position typically given to the weak, to the old, to the infirm, and, oftentimes, to women.

The girl, Elsa, did fine in position 3 for nearly a week, never underpainting or, worse, overpainting—whereby the poor deer looked like a tarted-up southern prostitute overcoming its grief with hard black tears—which was the real hazard of the job. No, the girl used the right amount of paint for the job, which allowed Clyde Sitwell, a thirty-year veteran of the plant and position 3's previous occupant, to be kept on permanent fire duty, the most coveted job on the line because it consisted of sitting beside the industrial fire extinguisher and reading the paper all day. Bob, as line foreman, was happy with the new arrangement: Clyde had been a notorious overpainter and would sometimes miss a deer or two, which left Bob in bed at night wondering about the fate of these poor animals, rooted to their post on some stranger's front lawn, blind in their one good eye with fear and easy prey for some larger, plastic animal.

4

Mary Edwards did not come to work one day. Her twin sons had come down with a volatile strain of chicken pox, their tongues, eyeballs, and lungs puffing up with the small fierce red dots, so Bob decided to take her spot at position 4 instead of reassigning everybody. What happened was this: The belt started moving at eight o'clock sharp; Bob grabbed his brush, dabbed some black paint, and watched the first fawn coming placidly down the line toward him; Charlie Wong, in position 1, attached the left antler as Walt Hiccama attached the right antler at the same exact time, the two of them like dancers in a strange, industrial choreography; the deer, with its small, noble antlers, paused for a moment between positions 3 and 4, where Bob dabbed the paint in its round socket, secretly feeling the miracle of life as the blackness quickly hardened into a shiny eye, and saw the girl, Elsa, do the same with one fancy swipe; and just as the fawn was headed to positions 5 and 6 for a dusting of white spots, the girl, the foreigner, began to sing:

"I am walking in the woods,
No, you are not there,
I walk among the dead,
Their eyes are full of tears."

On the next fawn, Bob used three times as much paint as needed, the girl's voice like a tiny, wilted violin whispering in his ears, and he could hear it, he could really hear it, even with his orange plastic earplugs in. "What are you doing?" Bob shouted over the heavy whirl of the conveyer belt at the girl.

"I am singing," she shouted back, dabbing another glob of black paint in place. Bob looked down, filled the next deer's eye, and listened as she continued:

"I am walking in the woods,
The forest is so dark,
I walk among the dead,
The trees are filled with arms."

Once again, he overpainted. He scooped off the excess paint with his fingers, leaving a terrible black streak down the fawn's nose. It was as if the factory were gone and the two of them, Bob and this tiny dark-eyed girl, were somewhere else, somewhere so quiet, in the middle of a snowstorm, and she was singing to him, she was singing to him to keep them both alive, because there was an avalanche of some kind, there was a glacier of white hanging over them both, and they were pressed together so tightly, and there was nothing around them but an abundance of white, the sound of everything was gone, all but her voice, this voice that was awful, really awful, but gentle in its own way. Just then he heard the conveyer grind to a halt, and the familiar red light that signaled a bottleneck on the line began to flash. He saw three deer piled, eyeless, lifeless, in front of him. It was in that moment, in that moment there, that Bob saw that he had been daydreaming, because he hadn't, no, he had not daydreamed in years.

5

At the Pilgrimtown junior varsity wrestling meet later that day, while hometown favorite Junior Williams, an enormous albino sophomore who wrecked the scales at nearly three hundred pounds, wrenched the dazed, gawking, freckled competition, some luckless freshman named Billy Grout, into the most dreaded fireman's carry, lifting the poor kid high into the sky before dropping him straight to the ground with what was usually the most satisfying sound heard all day, Bob realized he hardly cared. Even as the ref tore the boys apart, big Junior howling in fury and tearing at his opponent's nylon singlet like a wild animal, and even as the crowd saw that the freckled kid's arm was split like a matchstick, right in the middle, the heavy end of his hand dangling weak and broken like a flinted black head, all Bob could think about was hearing the girl sing again.

6

For the sake of productivity and quality on line 60, the next day Bob switched Owen Anders to position 4 and took Owen's job at position 7, adding the stripe of white to the animals' tails. It did not matter, though. Even four positions away, with the orange foam earplugs jammed hard into his ears, with his eyes planted firmly on the shiny puff of plastic that would, with one swab of white paint, be a deer tail, he could still make out her singing. He stamped his feet, he coughed, he pressed the earplugs all the way into his brain cavity, but still he could make out the words as clear as if she had been whispering them in his ear:

"*I have fallen for a soldier boy,*
A boy without a head,
I have fallen for a soldier boy,
My one true love is dead."

What kind of girl was this? From what kind of world? He could see her, alone, crowded in a thicket of bare trees and frost, surrounded by the arms and legs and burning uniforms of the recently deposed, the recently exploded, from some heinous civil war or some other factory fire, white skulls falling from the electric orange sky all around her like snow.

By lunchtime, Bob found he had to talk to her. In the break room, he stumbled around, clearing his throat. He stood, hovering beside where she sat, and saw she had taken off the brown hat of her uniform. Where the hat had been was the sheen of newly shorn hair, a few strands of brown silkiness a little longer than the rest fading in the white break room light. The girl was eating a dingy piece of white bread with a stain of yellow mustard on it, and finally, standing there, Bob thought to say, "You cut your hair?"

"I did." She squinted at him as though he were a child or an insane person, then went back to nibbling at her crumbly bread.

"Why did you cut it?" he asked.

"To sell. I make money for hair. I pay landlord for my heat."

He nodded and decided that was all he really wanted to know. He went to his usual spot in the break room, opened his lunch pail, and sat down across from Owen Anders, watching the horror of cheese and mayonnaise in the other man's gaping mouth and still wondering about everything.

7

That night in bed with his wife, he asked, "Did you ever stop and think, What am I doing all this for?"

"What, hun?" They were side by side, Bob lying on his back in his shorts, Patsy in curlers and a pink robe, reading a gory paperback mystery, with her back turned to him.

"Did you ever stop in the middle of something and say, 'What the heck did I waste fifteen years doing all of this for?'"

"Oh, like about twenty times a day," she laughed and turned, pinching his middle. She was an RN at the factory medical center. By the end of her shift, her ankles would be swollen large as melons. Bob frowned and looked away, feeling hurt.

"Oh dear, is this about the section foreman again?" she asked.

"No."

"Well, I said it before and I'll say it again. I think what they did to you was totally unfair. If anyone deserved that job, it was you. What line foreman has the best quality rates? What line foreman has the highest productivity? What line foreman has been more loyal to the company?"

"Nobody," Bob sighed.

"And that's why we all know you deserved that job more than anybody. And I'm sure, next year, when your review comes up again, you'll get it."

Bob nodded and turned on his side, facing the seashell-colored wall. It did not matter. The job did not matter. A promotion would not save him. Nothing like that mattered to him anymore.

8

In the middle of the Mold-o-Form union meeting, Bob suddenly wanted to stand up in front of everyone, all his friends, all his coworkers, the whole world of the plastics factory, to announce his big idea: the drawing he had made for a new lawn decoration, the one of the lovely doe nursing two of her wide-eyed young. But he did not. Instead, he finished collecting the union dues, placed the folded, mangled, mishandled cash in the shiny white lockbox, turned the key in the slot, and handed the box to Treasurer Simmky, who would count the cash and place it in the safe in the Mold-o-Form union office, where it would sit quietly until the end of the month, when all of the union's bills were paid. He nodded to Simmky, an oaf of a man with a square face like a dented pickup truck, then slipped the lockbox key back on his key ring. Bob thought once more about announcing his big idea, the mother deer and her young, but stopped himself, finding instead the comfort of a pink jelly doughnut.

9

At the end of one of the girl's songs the next day—"Burning, burning, burning from the cold . . . "—Bob knew at once that he would steal the money from the lockbox to give to the strange foreign girl. He was as sure of this as he was of the merit of his design for the mother deer and her two suckling babies. Somehow in his mind, it was part of the same thing, the need to do something good, to do something pretty.

What he thought would happen was this: He would steal the money and give it to the girl, she would disappear, Simmky would see the money was gone, and someone would immediately suspect the Mold-o-Form administration, someone like that fucker Mr. Bruin, who was antiunion and always coming up with ways to split it up, or maybe someone would lay blame on Simmky or maybe even on him, then a series of allegations would be made, the factory owners would be blamed because it was their office, their safe, their lack of security, and then the union members would elect to go on strike. Why? Because any reason was a good enough reason to avoid the factory for a day. Production would get backed up, decorative deer would lie in their molds, half formed, eyeless, tailless, without their happy white spots, collectible plates would go unetched and faceless, tiny green baby dolls would go without their heads, consumers would call and complain, someone from the administration would make a speech, the union would stand strong, the factory and then the town would grind to a halt, the massive presses would finally go quiet, the green vapor would no longer rise, people would hear the nervous, joyful whispers they had been uttering to each other their whole lives, plastics would be considered a thing of the past, the factory would close, a forest would grow in its place, and somehow things would change, things would really change.

Bob fingered the lockbox key in his pocket and knew he would do it by the end of the day.

After work and outside the corrugated metal warehouse for Fannie the Fawn, Bob took the girl's small white hand in his own, gently opened her fingers, and placed the hot bundle of cash in her palm. He looked at her, really looked at her for the first time: the short snub nose, the dark gray circles under the dark, hopeless eyes, the lips that were chapped and rigid and doubtful of everything. He looked at her, then let go of her hand and waited. He waited for all the presses in the whole world of Pilgrimtown to be quiet, to be hushed by the huff and release of their own phosphorescent green steam, and then he said, "Go away. Go far away from here. Take a plane back to wherever you came from and don't ever come back here again."

Beneath the hood of her dirty white winter jacket, the girl's brown eyes got big, big and, for one moment, not brown but a kind of flecked green, a kind of lovely shiny green like two planets made entirely of gas, and then she turned her fist into a tiny knot, looked over her shoulder, and ran for the gates. Her hood flapping as she moved, spouts of her breath turning to fog, the sound of her feet in snow soft and unstopping, she disappeared into the employee parking lot and was gone and it was true. It was the most beautiful, most decent thing Bob had seen since he couldn't remember when. In a moment, Bob turned back toward the entrance, and without looking he knew. The factory was on fire again.

A TRIP TO GREEK MYTHOLOGY CAMP

1

In the mail, from an ad she had found in *Christian Wife's Pious Housekeeping,* my mother received a brochure for the Teen Institute Training and Nature camp. She'd sent away for it, with the Holy Ghost's permission, to keep me from another summer dedicated to Dungeons and Dragons and huffing Carbona carpet cleaner. Last summer there had been an incident where I had disappeared for two days and was found sleeping in the backseat of my mother's station wagon with Magic Marker on my chest that read I AM GALDAR THE DESTROYER after a particularly intense gaming session one evening.

2

"TITAN," the brochure read in bold letters with a silver thunderbolt and gold chariot exploding through the middle of a formidable Greek-inspired font. The brochure described a monthlong summer camp where teens could meet other teens with similar interests in history, arts and crafts, and Greek mythology, all in a beautiful and safe natural Ohio woodland setting. "The camp will work to foster your teen's self-confidence and allow for the development of ever necessary social skills"—which in my case were definitely lacking. In the glossy brochure there were color photos of a handsome boy, slick as an eel, swimming in a false blue lake; another of a beautiful young blond girl working at a ceramics wheel making an impossibly intricate urn; and another of two good-looking teenagers, a boy and a girl who could have been television stars, with smiles like denture ads, dressed in white tunics, drinking from gold goblets, and laughing. "Does your teen have a hard time fitting in?" the brochure read. "Why not go to a camp where meeting other like-minded, intelligent teens is easy?" My mother handed the brochure to my father, nodding her head and smiling. "What do you think, son?" she asked me.

"Okay," I said. My father looked at the brochure, then at me, and walked out of the house sighing. In a moment, like an argument, we could hear things breaking in the garage and then the sound of the lawn mower starting.

3

I had drawn a dirty picture of a girl. The girl in the picture was someone I had fallen in love with in my high school history class. I had never spoken to her. She was a redhead, and her name was Madeline. Some girls in class called her Maddie. The picture was taken away from me in class and then sent home to my parents. Seeing it, they at once realized the worst of their fears: there really was something wrong with me. And perhaps my dad, being a man, had secretly gathered from the anatomically retarded drawing that I, at the age of sixteen, was still a virgin or, worse, a budding homo. "This is unacceptable, Josh, unacceptable" was all they could say. The look of disappointment on my father's sturdy gray face was equal to the way he had received news of my brother losing his entire left leg the year before in a training accident in the army.

4

"I heard you were going to geek vasectomy camp," Eric Peters shouted as I turned down the block on my bike, home from school for the day. Eric Peters lived across the street; he had red freckles and was two years younger than me, an eighth grader. All of Eric Peters's brothers were wrestlers. All of them were big and tough. Eric wasn't big yet, but he was tough. He would wear his older brother's ear pads and singlet around the neighborhood, a red and white wrestling leotard with matching headpiece, and try to practice his wrestling moves on me.

"It's mythology camp," I shouted back. "It's about Greek gods."

"Can I borrow your bike while you're gone?" he asked.

"I guess."

"Can I try it out now?"

"All right," I said. I hopped off and handed it to him. The bike had been a birthday present last year. It was gold and black and had a thunderbolt on the frame. Eric hopped on, rode it around a little, and nodded. "Not bad, not bad," he said. Then he sped off down the block, turned, and began pedaling as fast as he could right toward me. I knew what was going to happen before it did. Eric's beady black eyes squinted tight as he let out a howl—"Eric Peters is number one!"—and at the last moment he hopped off the bike, dove into the grass, and laughed as the front tire of my bike slammed hard against a tree.

"Ghosted!" Eric shouted.

"That's great," I said, lifting up the bike. The handlebars were bent all the way to the left, and one of the forks had a very large dent. "Great," I said and sighed, walking away. Eric Peters, you foolish mortal, I thought. You have made a deadly foe, a deadly foe this day. I imagined sewing him up in a burlap sack with hundreds of cloves of garlic and dropping him over the city walls to a pack of hungry wild dogs, or decapitating him and mounting his head on a great gold lance. As I was fantasizing, I heard, "Eric Peters is number one!" and suddenly he surprise attacked me with a full nelson I could not contend.

5

In the picture I had drawn in class, the girl was naked and her back was turned. In class, the girl sat two rows ahead of me, and all I could do was imagine how she would look naked like that, the soft slope of the back of her long white neck, her shoulders only hinting at her warm, soft curves. In the picture, her hair was almost black. It was done entirely with lead pencil. The thing was, though, there was a man in the picture who had a large horse head instead of a man's head. And a sword. He was holding the sword and leaping naked atop Madeline, whose long white arms reached up to embrace him. Tears of joy flew from the side of Madeline's face, and the man with the horse head was also inexplicably crying. I didn't really know why I drew them crying. My mother asked if either one of them was in pain. I shook my head. "They're just in love," I said.

6

At the camp, I got off the sour-milk-smelling bus and followed the rest of the kids into a large wood cabin with a sign in gold letters that read ZEUS CABIN—HEAD COUNSELOR ONLY. I had hives from the black vinyl seat creeping up and down the back of my legs, and I hadn't eaten since that morning. "Okay," said the camp leader—DAVE was on his name badge—"how many of you kids have ever been to any kind of summer camp before?" A chubby, red-faced boy, a girl with a baseball hat on, and an Asian kid in overalls raised their hands. Dave nodded. He was thin and bearded and had wild brown hair that was longer in the back. He wore a gold cardboard laurel wreath above his ears and a short purple tunic, which showed his knobby knees. A silver whistle dangled from his neck. He was thin but had large calves, and he shifted his weight from leg to leg as he spoke. "Okay," he said, "this place . . . well, this place is going to be a lot different. Here we wear tunics and stay up late. So it's going to be better, a lot better than . . . well, anything."

7

TITAN probably had been a great summer camp when it first opened in the fifties, but now it was as dingy and wrecked as a sunken ship. In the center of the camp was a great coliseum made completely of wood, but it hadn't been painted in years and was dusty with paint chips. One side had fallen in on itself and had been graffitied with black paint that said SUCK IT! and EAT PUSSY! There were stone carvings of Greek gods and heroes and monsters—Hercules, Hermes, the Hydra, Medusa—hiding in the dense woods along the paths, but they had been grown over with mossy filth or had broken or missing arms and noses or worse. The statue of Eros, the god of love, was covered with eight or nine brightly colored condoms. The outhouse was lit up pink and named the Oracle. It had flashing lights, and speakers piped harp music inside, but most of the speakers had been blown and now only crackled with wiry fuzz.

"I'll be honest. We have a problem here at TITAN," Dave announced at the opening day meeting. "Transients and migrant workers and Mexicans. They all camp here during the off months. They stay here so they can work at the paper factory, and they make a goddamn mess of the place," he shouted. Then he lowered his head, and his laurel wreath tipped shamefully. "So every night two kids will be on patrol. They'll have this flashlight to use." He held up a shiny silver flashlight and shook it. "And this whistle. If you see any transients, just blow the whistle and flash the light in their eyes. They can't stand the light. Also, we're low on supplies, so if you can get away with one piece of toilet paper, well, that would be nice."

8

The boys were all instructed to meet down by the lake on the first day. The lake was green and covered in fuzzy yellow and white moss. A few weak-looking willows hovered over the shoreline in a sad circle. "All right, then, everyone take off your clothes," Dave shouted, blowing on the whistle. "It's time to commune with the Greek god Neptune."

"What?" the Asian kid asked, holding his hand to his ear as if he hadn't heard right.

"Take off your clothes right now, Asian kid, and go for a swim," Dave instructed again. He blew the whistle, took a seat on the shore, and began digging at his palm for a splinter that seemed to be bothering him. The Asian kid shook his head, but no one else argued. The Asian kid just stood there for a moment and watched, and I stared back at him, feeling more uncomfortable than I had in all my life. As the teenage boys around me began to disrobe and their soft white bellies and acne-scarred spines began to appear, I bent over and began unbuckling my pants as well. Out of the corner of my eye, out of curiosity, I glanced at the naked boys around me. The Asian kid sighed and finally began lifting off his shirt, muffling his crying. In another moment, however, we were all in the water and splashing about, and it was if we had been born that way, naked, amphibious, daring. The Asian kid floated on his back and seemed to be smiling.

9

On the second night in the dank, mildewed cabin that was named Hercules, which was written in silver cursive just above the entranceway, I lay in bed and listened to a flute being played somewhere. When I couldn't sleep, I climbed out of the bunk and stood by the foggy glass window. Outside, older boys and girls in white tunics tied tightly with gold cords were chasing one another and laughing. A tall girl with brown hair came running past the window, and a boy with dark eyes and a budding mustache came after her. He grabbed her around her middle as she let out a laugh, and he began kissing her neck. I turned away and then turned back again, and his hand had disappeared somewhere along her middle. Just then, along the side of the girls' cabin, Cassidy Ponce appeared, a short blond girl with glasses who I decided I loved right away. After a chance encounter outside the craft hall, where she accidentally stabbed me with a pair of safety scissors, I had been watching her. Now there, outside the girls' cabin, some older boy with mop-cut hair was trying to kiss her openmouthed. But Cassidy Ponce just kneed him once in the groin and marched away, tilting her head back and laughing loudly.

10

"I want to be sent home right away," the Asian kid, George, shouted. "If my parents knew what was going on here . . . " He stood up in the middle of the dining hall—the Kingdom of Demeter—and threw down his fork.

Dave, itching his light brown beard, came over and patted the boy on his back. "Well, Asian kid, here we settle things with the sword," he whispered, nodding wisely. He walked over to a wall and removed a heavy silver broadsword and handed it to the boy, then turned and chose for himself a great spiked mace.

"What?" the boy whimpered.

"If you want to go home, you'll have to best me. Go on, Asian kid, best me! Best me!"

The boy thought for a moment, trying to lift the sword, then shook his head and let it drop. Dave lowered his mace, patted the boy on the back, and walked away.

11

"In the spirit of ancient Greece, a land in which all of you would already be married, today you will be assigned your husband or wife for the remainder of your time here at camp. If you have not already chosen one, one will be chosen for you. Tony Briggs, you'll be with Cassidy Ponce. Mark Malloy, you'll be with Angie McGribbs. Josh Lundton, you'll be married to Lucy Anders. Ares cabin, you'll be with the girls from Aphrodite cabin. Argonaut cabin, you'll pair up with the Wood Nymph cabin. John Ford—sorry, pal, but we ran out of girls, so you'll be married to me."

12

All the girls were instructed to spend the night with their husbands for at least the first night. The girl, Lucy, who had been chosen as my wife was sixteen, brunette, and a diabetic. She warned me not to offer her any kind of candy whatsoever, then laughed and patted down her heavily-hair-sprayed hair. She also had a wicked-bad case of eczema, this river of bright red sores that ran from one corner of her mouth all the way down her throat. She was skinny and lay in bed beside me, silent, trembling, and waiting in a pink football jersey, which I guessed had been her older brother's but had been ruined in the laundry. She closed her eyes and pulled at the corner of the jersey. I looked at her and placed my hand between us, wanting and not wanting all of the same things at the same time. Finally, I chickened out and pretended to fall asleep, and Lucy huffed and turned over and kicked me several times during the night.

"In the Elysian Mysteries, Hades, the god of the underworld, falls in love with Persephone, a human girl, and kidnaps her and tricks her into eating a pomegranate seed from the land of the dead, which means she has to go back to the underworld for part of the year for all eternity."

One night out on camp patrol alone, I go to the Oracle-themed outhouse and struggle looking for toilet paper. I find this myth in its entirety scratched into the bottom side of one of the toilet seats. I think it might mean that no matter what, you can't change certain things. Or maybe you can change certain things. I am not sure, though, because like all the Greek myths, it might mean anything.

Minutes later, as I stumble out, I run into Cassidy Ponce, the short, perky blond girl with huge bifocal cat-eye glasses, the girl I have been "watching from afar" all week. "Hey," she says. "You're in Tony's cabin, right? Hercules cabin?"

"I think so. Tony, the guy with long hair in the back? Or short, fat Tony?"

"With the hair in the back." She smiles. "I go to high school with him in Grand Rapids."

"You do?" I ask.

"Yeah. I guess that's why they made me marry him."

"You're married to him?"

"Yeah. It's not so bad. He keeps his hands off me because he knows I've got friends who'll kick his ass."

"What are you—I mean, what is a girl like you doing here?" I blurt out suddenly.

"I don't know." She frowns and pushes her huge glasses up her nose. "I heard they had a unicorn."

"A unicorn?"

"Yeah. Come look." She takes my hand—her hand so small, like a child's—and we run through the dark, down a path, me breathing hard. We stop before a huge white concrete statue of a unicorn, its pointy head lowered sadly.

"It's a grave marker," she says and points to the etched lettering.

"A grave marker? You mean they had a real unicorn here?" I ask.

"Back in the seventies, you know? They took a miniature horse and grafted an antelope horn on its head. Its name was Hermes."

"Like the Greek messenger?"

"Right. It used to tour around with the circus, and then some animal rights group found out and so they had to keep it here. It died only last year."

"Wow," I say, sad that that's all I can come up with.

"And, well . . . Forget it," she says.

"No, go on," I say.

"In China there's evidence that there really used to be unicorns. They think they were hunted to extinction."

"Really?"

"Really. I have like eight hundred books about them at home."

"Unicorns are cool. I guess I'm more into the heroes and monsters, Cyclops, stuff like that," I say.

"Yeah, I kinda figured," she says.

"So," I say.

"So. Do you have any friends who like this kind of stuff back home?" she asks.

"No. I don't think anybody here does."

"Yeah." She laughs and pushes up her glasses. "You're probably right."

"What about you?" I ask. "You got a cool jock boyfriend or anything?"

"No, no. I got a neighbor who's like a senior who comes over and makes out with me." She pushes up her glasses. "I know he just does it to piss his real girlfriend off. . . . But this conversation is getting very interesting, huh?"

"Yeah," I say.

"Well, so I'll say it. I'm still a virgin. It's not like I'm a freak about it or anything, I just don't really date, I guess," she says.

"Well, sure," I say. "I get it."

She pushes up her glasses again.

"So do you want to take a walk down by the lake or something?" I ask.

"I don't think I should."

"You don't think you should?"

"I don't think I should. I'm married to someone else. In ancient Greece, if a woman was caught with another man, she'd have her genitals torn out and pulled up over her head."

I can't tell if she is joking or not. I touch her shoulders and feel the heavy material of the white tunic in my hands. In my life I have never touched another person so gently.

"But . . . ," I whisper.

"I am married to someone else," she whispers again and this time closes her eyes to be kissed.

HAPPINESS WILL BE YOURS

1

Outside the gates, Billy does not hesitate to hug me. Right in the entranceway to the Kiddieland Amusement Park, right in the middle of the gleaming black parking lot, with God and the overweight parking lot attendant both watching, God invisible, the attendant in his yellow uniform riding his little motorized golf cart and, seeing two grown men holding each other like this, turning up his eyes in a very suspicious look. Right there among the crowds and crowds of howling youngsters with melted candy on their hands and worn-out parents arguing with each other about ever getting married, fighting about how the husband may or may not have flirted with the teenage ticket taker, and past them the sparkling rows of blue and gray and green station wagons, parked neat and distressed like at some failing car dealership, and in the distance, looming, the enormous pink grinning head of everybody's favorite pink cartoon bunny, Lloyd the Rabbit, who is smiling a gigantic cartoon speech bubble that says WELCOME TO THE LAND OF HAPPINESS. KIDS $8, ADULTS $15. In front of all this and everybody, Billy grabs me around the neck, quickly, desperately.

Another year has gone by, and Billy is still as short as ever. His hair is dark and greasy. His eyes twitch nervously beneath his big black bifocal glasses, which are taped along one side of the frames. With his small face against my collar, I suddenly know I can't go on doing this anymore. I can't because, as it turns out, he is crying already.

2

Outside the gates we get two adult passes. A teenage girl with a mild case of acne on her forehead, big doe eyes that make you just wish you were sixteen again, and a name tag that reads SHAWNA stares at me curiously. When I tell Billy that I got it, that I'll pay for both tickets, he hugs me again. The ticket taker asks, "How many kids?" and I say, "Just the two adults is all." She snaps her blue bubble gum and hands me the two tickets, staring at my face as if she is memorizing it, thinking how she will describe it later to a very interested police sketch artist. *He had a cut under one eye and short brown hair and a cunning sort of nose and an extremely weak mouth,* I imagine her saying. Then snap goes the gum again. I take the tickets and whiz through the turnstile. Billy is still thanking me, and all this time he has not stopped touching me. His hand is on my shoulder, or his arm is around my neck, or he is ruffling my hair. I take notice of this as we walk past a smiling, costumed, life-size Lloyd the Rabbit, whose job it is to greet people and who comes close to hug me. I stick my arm out in a very defensive gesture, shoving the poor rabbit away. The rabbit, who is probably just some unlucky teenager, hops back, cowering behind his big pink mitts. Billy sees this all happen and whispers in my ear, hand on my shoulder again, "You've finally given up on all that meditation and anger management junk, haven't you?"

3

Our deal was this: On the last day of summer vacation, the one right before we both went into fourth grade, Billy and I got abducted by a man who lived two blocks away, in the last house by the woods, right before Cherry Lane. The man drove up to the end of Billy's driveway, where we were playing horse. He opened the back door of his beige and brown Dodge station wagon and lifted out two brand-new twelve-inch Atom Man figurines, the kind that had been sold out for weeks. One was Blaine Bridges as a news reporter that could be transformed into Atom Man, and the other was Gort, Blaine's robot bodyguard/butler/chauffeur. Seeing the toys immediately made a small and envious wound in the center of my heart. The man motioned to us with his long white hand, and Billy, being trusting—the way he was and never would be again—walked right up to him, and I followed, both of us staring. The man asked, "Do either of you fellas like Atom Man?"

Billy nodded frantically, nervously. He pushed his tiny black glasses up his nose and took a step closer.

"Would either one of you like a free Atom Man?"

Billy nodded slower, pushing up his glasses once more and stepping closer again. I didn't move. I stared at the man and asked, "How come?"

The man frowned, then drew a small smile on his pink lips and said, "Because today's your lucky day."

"But why?"

"What can I say, kiddo? I work for the toy company. We want to know what your favorite toy is."

"Well, it's the Blue Falcons. Atom Man's okay, but do you got a Blue Falcon Fighting Squadron leader?"

"Nah, I don't think so."

"We went to buy Blue Falcon, but everyone's sold out of him," Billy said.

"Well, why don't you try these two out and see what you think?"

"If we wait and don't take anything now, can you bring us a Blue Falcon later?" I asked.

"Why not take these now, and I can come back with the other ones. How's that?"

"So we get both then? Because I'd rather just wait if we only get one," I said.

"Sure," he said. "You can get both. Just come and take these now."

"Nah, I'll just wait, I guess," I said.

"Yeah, I'll wait, too," Billy said.

"Look, there's a heap of toys in the back here. Why don't you just pick one out, and I'll bring you whatever you want later? Okay? How's that? Just pick one out."

Before I could say anything, Billy had already climbed into the backseat. When the man reached around and grabbed Billy by his neck, shoving him inside, all Billy said was, "Hey, mister, you just broke my glasses."

4

Here's one for you then: The woman I'm in love with, who is not the woman I married, lives in the apartment upstairs with a nice enough guy named Larry, whose only crime in the world was to move into the Royal Arcade apartment building where I happened to be living. Larry works nights as a shift manager at Dinky Donut down the street. There are powdered sugar footprints everywhere in their place and always a few dozen miniature glazed doughnuts sitting in a bowl on the fridge. I eat them and wonder if Larry has any idea what his wife and I do while he's away. The woman, his wife, her name is Jean and she is a veterinarian and she often misplaces her glasses. Sometimes I steal them so she'll have a reason to come downstairs and visit me. Her husband thinks that she and I are on a bowling team. Really, though, we sit on my sofa and hold hands and stare out the window and pretend that we did not make major mistakes in our lives and that instead of her and Larry it is her and me that are married. In bed I say, "Are you a good wife or a bad wife?" Sometimes she slides an imaginary ring on my finger. In the middle of all that, I sometimes feel a kind of hole open up, and I know that somewhere something terrible is happening to somebody.

5

At the top of Splash-A-Way Mountain, which is fake blue water and fake molded brown rocks and yet still very peaceful, still very serene, I am buckled into a foamy black seat, a restraint bar locked across my chest. Billy turns to me, worried, a long look on his small face, and says, "I'm getting divorced again.

Yep. Number two, just like that. What a surprise, right? Sure, right down the goddamn tubes." His glasses are already wet with water. His face is sweaty. It does not seem that he ever stops crying.

"Yeah? Divorced? Billy, that's too bad. Well, welcome to the club," I say, not surprised so much as sad that this marriage has not worked out either.

"I've pretty much given up. I've pretty much given up on everything," he says as we crest over the rapids. Billy is crying again, and then everything is silenced by our falling.

6

Our dream is the thing that haunts me. In the basement where we were kept for four days—where the floor was covered in dirt because the man had torn through the foundation of his house and had dug five small graves, two of which were already filled and one which was larger than the rest, just his size—the only light was from a yellow-caged utility bulb, the kind you might find carpenters using, that was left planted in the ground like a brilliant glowing flower. Billy and I sat back-to-back, duct-taped together, our hands, our knees, our feet, our necks stuck, only two of my fingers managing to push through, touching the dirt, which was wet almost, the feeling of the dirt being the only feeling of comfort I could find. Billy cried for four days straight, the mucus high and full in his voice, whining about *his broken glasses, his broken glasses,* because we were allowed to talk and were told we would live as long as we were quiet. By the second day, though, I was sure we were going to die, because I could see fine, and I was the one facing the open graves. The man had already placed my shoes and Billy's broken glasses inside two separate holes, and he would lumber past us as if we were ghosts already and continue his digging. When he was in some other part of the house and the room was filled with the familiar sound of crickets outside and police sirens, Billy began praying, promising to do better, to stop fucking around at school, to pay attention in church, to not break his glasses anymore, to stop walking in on his older sister, accidentally on purpose, I guess. By the third day both of us began swearing up a storm, because no one was there to stop us, and we made retarded combinations of swearwords, like "superfuckass" and "uglybitchwad." Eventually, we wet our pants and ruined the ground around us with the smell of our own waste. Then, soon enough, came Billy's dream, and it was this dream that still haunted me. We would be saved somehow, and we would go to the Kiddieland Amusement Park every weekend. They would let us ride all the rides for free and maybe even close down the park just for us, because when some little girl fell down a well in the town over from ours, that's what they did for her when she got out. Also, Billy was going to eat candy for a week—morning, noon, and night, nothing but candy, mostly chocolate saltwater taffy, and go to Toytown and pick out whatever he wanted. Then he was going to throw a brick through Mr. Altamont's front window for backing over Billy's new BMX racing bike, the Viper. Mr. Altamont had backed over it on purpose, because Billy had been warned. We both saw it happen, and Mr. Altamont had definitely been smiling.

7

"So you're not going to call him back?" Jean asks as we are lying in bed and the two of us are smoking. According to Jean, this is the only time it is okay for us to smoke, so we do, sharing a cigarette, which I smoke most of anyway. I like that she worries about my smoking. My ex-wife would watch me smoke cigarette after cigarette and sigh, turning back to the TV.

"I don't think I want to see him this year." I turn over, and Jean loops her bare leg over me. Beneath the white sheet, she pinches my side and moves her hand along my chest.

"You should at least call him back."

"I just don't want to talk to him," I say, and she begins gently scratching the back of my head.

"Maybe he just wants to talk. He needs somebody to talk with." Immediately, I see Jean, twelve, blond hair in pigtails, holding two scrawny and denuded pink baby birds in a pouch she has made by lifting up the ends of her shirt, and she is nuzzling them against her chest. "Maybe he's just lonely."

"I'll call him, I'll call him," I say, and she says, "You're so good. You're such a good husband." She is kissing me, and she is soft all over, and we are going to do what a man and wife would do, but I will not enjoy it because I am thinking now. I am thinking that out of all the promises I have ever made—like my own lousy, failed marriage, like promising to pay the money back to my dad that he lent me for college but that I blew on a piece-of-shit Camaro, and all the hundreds of promises between God and me, and maybe the one between me and Billy, the only one I ever thought I'd be able to keep—here I am, kissing someone else's wife and telling her that I'll call, but all the time I know I'm lying.

8

We make it once a month for the first year. The owners of Kiddieland, who at the time are suffering very terrible losses due to the new Rocket Falls Waterslide Park that has opened just down the street, see Billy and me as a great source of publicity, and the first Saturday of every month, between twelve and one, the park closes, and Billy and I get to ride whatever rides we want for free. Mostly, it is on the workers' lunch break, and some heavy with keys follows us around and operates the rides we want to go on. He stands there bored and smoking and wondering what two scrawny white kids ever did to be treated so special, but of course he knows, because everybody who works there for a few weeks or so knows. We are given all the cotton candy we can eat and special laminated gold passes that we flash to the ticket taker at the gate. Our names are written on them in calligraphy, along with MEMBERS FOR LIFE, IN PERPETUITY. Once, Billy vomited for an hour after riding the Hurricane five times straight, and another time I drank so much soda that I couldn't stop laughing for anything. That is until new owners, Serbians, bought the place, and one Saturday when we flashed our gold passes, they were taken away. A man with a heavy black mustache tried to explain the situation, but by then we were getting older and thinking about boning girls, stuff like that, and, well, it went from once a month to every few and then to once a year. But Billy wouldn't let it go past that. Once a year he'd call me up, persistent—in high school, college, and even when he moved out of state. He got a job as a teacher for a while, got fired, got work as an office manager, but no matter what, he always remembered to call. We usually went on the first weekend of August. We missed only one year, the year my mom died, which happened right around that time. Billy showed up at the funeral, patted me on the back, and in the middle of the wake or wherever it was, said something like, "We'll go there twice next year."

9

At the intersection of Soda Pop Town and Hot Dog Junction, where surly teenagers in pink rabbit visors serve us jumbo rabbit-head-shaped onion rings, I try to tell Billy that I don't want to do this again. I try to tell him that I'm too old and that the past is just the past and that I need to move on and that maybe it's harmful psychologically. I haven't wanted to come in years, but I do, and I can't do it anymore. But all that comes out is, "That new Typhoon coaster is something, huh? Man, these kids don't know how good they got it. Whew."

"Man, we woulda rode that coaster all summer, you know? Remember that old wooden one, the Wild Bull? Now that was a coaster. I thought for sure when I came over that hill and it turned, man, I was sure I was gonna fly out each time. Wow. There are a lot of memories here, a lot of memories."

"Sure," I say. "Sure."

"I mean, this is the only place where everything's good for me, you know?"

"Sure, I do, sure," I say, and it's at that exact moment, with him dipping his big rabbit-head onion ring in a pile of my ketchup, with the cackle of kids being spun around the roller coaster track at a million miles an hour behind me, that I know I won't ever be coming back again.

10

In the photo they gave the police psychic who finally found us, it is Halloween, I am six and Billy is five, and we are both sitting in a red metal wagon. I am dressed up as a lion and already eating some of my candy. Billy is a cowboy, and, like usual, he is crying. The way my mom tells it, the psychic held the photo in her two hands, then placed it against her heart and said, "This one, this little cowboy, is very sad." Billy's mom let out a howl followed by a series of hand-wringing sobs. The psychic then held the photo to her forehead and said, "They are near an amusement park. They are near a place with roller coasters."

"Are they both still alive?" my mother asked.

"For now," the psychic said. "But I see them in darkness. Covered in dirt. Hurry, you must hurry." For two more days they searched around the nearest amusement parks, carnivals, and even the video arcade, all in vain. On the fourth night, my mother woke up to the telephone and screamed through the dark for it to "please, God, keep ringing."

"I have found your son," a strange voice announced.

"Who is this?" my mother howled.

"Greta, the police psychic."

"Where? Where is he?" my mother asked.

"He keeps on crying. I keep hearing it. When I was sleeping, in the shower, at the grocery store. So I drove around until it got louder. I can show you the house. It's over on Cherry. By the woods."

"Oh my God, my God. . . . Please, please show me," my mother whispered.

"First of all, your kid is the one who cries all the time, right? I called you first because, well, I hate to say it, but I think the other one is dead."

11

Of course, as I am trying to think of the words to tell Billy that I am not going to meet him again next year, there is an argument that happens among the happy, brightly colored aisles of Toytown that goes exactly like this:

Billy: Do you have twenty bucks I can borrow?

Me: Yeah. What for?

Billy: This kid, the clerk behind the counter, says he knows where I can get some blow.

Me: Blow? You mean like cocaine?

Billy: Yeah. Yeah. He says he knows somebody.

Me: Yeah, Bill, I don't think that's what you need right now.

Billy: Yeah, maybe not, but what the hell. Can you spot me?

Me: Not for that.

Billy: Okay, how about ten then?

Me: That's not the point.

Billy: How'd it come out that you are all hunky-dory and my life is total shit?

And then, as you might expect, he starts crying.

Billy: I don't want to be alive anymore, Georgie.

Me: Don't say that kind of stuff, man. It'll be okay. It'll be all right.

Billy: You know what? That's what you said last year. You don't even be-lieve the shit you say, man.

Me: I believe it. But you gotta believe it, too, man.

Billy: You can't tell me you believe it, man. You can't tell me you believe it. . . .

He lets out a heavy sob, shaking his head and moaning.

Me: Here, Billy, take a deep breath. Hand me your glasses and wipe your face, man.

And he hands over the dirty black frames. I am in awe and terror, realizing they are the same exact worn-out ones from when we were kids.

12

At the Fudgepot, after a dozen or so gobs of chocolate and marshmallow dipped in milky fondue, I go and call Jean. Billy has run to the bathroom, warning me that he might need a couple minutes in there. "Colon trouble," he says with a laugh. "I need to go see a specialist or something while I'm still on the wife's insurance."

I dial Jean's number, and when Larry answers, I just cough.

"Yeah, Larry. This is George. From downstairs. Is, um, Jean in?"

"Yeah, man. You guys have bowling tonight?"

"No. We were going to scrimmage another team from the alley, but I have this date with this bimbo. Tits out to here. You know how it is."

"Sure, pal. Give 'em a squeeze for me. Hang on." He mumbles something else, then hands the phone to Jean.

"So did you tell him yet?" Jean asks right away.

"Not yet."

"See. That's good. Deep down you know how much he needs you."

"No, that wasn't it. He just started telling me about his divorce, and, well, I dunno."

"He's getting divorced?" she asks, the tenderness becoming soft, so soft in her voice. At that moment, I want to be anywhere but where I am, far away with Jean, in a new life, with a job that doesn't involve me smiling behind a customer service desk in a stupid red vest, in an apartment where I don't have to listen to the creaking upstairs wondering if Jean and Larry are kissing or worse. I want to be on another planet and not who I am, but I don't say any of this. I just go: "Jean, I don't got anything good but you. And you aren't even mine really."

There is silence for a while, and then she says, "I gotta go. Stop by later. And say hi to your friend for me."

Outside Mr. Altamont's house, we sit and smoke in my car. The blue light from Mr. Altamont's TV flickers on the big front window, still perfectly intact. We chicken out most times. One year when we were teenagers, I guess, Billy threw a brick and broke a blue ceramic window planter, missing the window completely. A few years ago when he got fired from his job teaching, he walked right up to the Altamonts' porch and tossed a tire iron as hard as he could and busted the hell out of the window, but no one did anything. Mrs. Altamont had

BLUEBIRDS USED TO CROON IN THE CHOIR

48

had a stroke the week before, and Mr. Altamont was sitting beside her in the hospital. The two of us just stared at the broken glass and then walked back to the car, quietly.

In the dark, no one is saying anything. I think of Jean, and maybe Billy is crying again, so I say, "Man, I gotta tell you. I can't even blame it. I can't blame it on what happened anymore." I blurt it out suddenly. I cough up some smoke, and my eyes water from it.

"Yeah, me either, I guess," he says. I look over at him, then at the window.

"Sometimes I get the feeling I just want to forget it, you know?"

"Yeah," he says.

"Like maybe I should be thankful, you know? Thankful I'm halfway okay."

"Yeah."

I look at the window again. "So maybe not this year, huh, Billy?"

"Maybe not, man."

"So," I say.

"So." There is silence then. Billy is never silent, so I get nervous and blurt out, "Well, so, you want to go meet the lady I'm in love with?"

"Okay. Yeah," he says.

"She's married to this other dude, but, well, what the hell."

"What the hell is right," he says. "You gotta take what you can get."

For no real reason then, as I pull the crappy blue Ford away, I turn on the radio. "Baba O'Reilly" by the Who is on. *Bawww—bowww—bawww.* I turn it up and start doing the air guitar parts, real big, singing along, and Billy is crying to himself but smiling. I just start honking like crazy.

BE A GOOD CITIZEN

1

Summer meant secrets to be set apart for Emily. She was eleven now, going into seventh grade over at the Madame Lewis School, and would spend each morning of her summer vacation on the roof of the apartment house, helping to tend to Mr. Butter's beautiful white carrier pigeons: feeding, training, and tying the tiny, elusive messages to the small red leather binders on their legs. Mr. Butter had a "lady friend" over in Huntley County to whom he would send short, hand-scrawled notes ("You are as sweet as a plate of sugar apple dumplings" or "Kiss-kiss, hug-hug from your Big Ball of Butter" or simply "Be mine, won't you, hunny?"). The woman he was courting was named Hazel, and Mr. Butter claimed she was just a year younger, only eighty-two, and was as fair and charming as the face of a country daisy. The summer was one quiet stretch of morning, and Emily, who still wore her school uniform, a gray linen skirt, would lie on her back and watch the powdery birds sweep above her in great circular patterns, dozens and dozens of tiny white puffs gently following Mr. Butter's graceful whistles and commands.

But today there was trouble in the pigeon coop. It had begun last night with a terrible womanlike scream, the sound a startled lady might make on a crime program on the radio or on TV. It had happened around midnight and had reoccurred all morning.

The birds were frantic now, clawing at the wire, hissing and flapping their dirty white and brown and gray wings, trampling one another as they swooped about their small, tightly locked wooden pens, their eyes black and grave, mouths clasping and unclasping, for none of the birds had been fed for three days or more, perhaps as long ago as Sunday.

Emily pried and pried at the wooden cage door, but there were two locks on it, ever since Dusty Evans, a boy on the fourth floor of the apartment house, and his two pals had broken into the pen a year ago and stolen some eggs to drop off the roof at unlucky people passing by. The female pigeons, whose eggs had been taken, sat in their nests the rest of the summer, searching about, unwilling to leave for fear their brood might somehow return, not understanding that their young were gone and dead. The females had to be killed come autumn, for they would not eat or take out on their own, and Emily saw the consequences first-hand of what was commonly called, through the whispering vents all around the apartment house, a trial of heartache.

Emily's own mother had had a bout of it herself. A washerwoman and cleaning lady, Emily's mother had been left holding the most precarious kind of dirty bundle, a baby, while her no-account man took a job as a teletypist in Poughkeepsie. Their apartment was dark and empty, like a spook house at the carnival, haunted with the flapping bedsheets and silky pajamas and unmatched socks and secondhand evening gowns of other neighborhood souls dancing like phantom ballerinas all around. There were the royal green stockings of the schoolteacher, Mrs. Andress; the milkman's white uniform, pressed and ironed; Dr. Gelding's shiny black pants, which Emily recognized from when she had run a fever and he had checked her temperature by holding her forehead as she sat on his lap. Many kinds of clothing hung from every curtain rod, every floor lamp, so that although during the summer Emily's mother was away at work, scrubbing elevators and stairwells most of the day, because of all the strange shapes of the familiar clothes, which became neighbors in their own way, Emily hardly ever felt lonely. It was like a tea party every afternoon with the most well-behaved guests from all along the street, and Emily, alone at the table, sipped tea and asked Mrs. Plum's billowy purple gown if she preferred one sugar or two or if she would like cream perhaps. When she did feel lonesome or worried, it was off to Mr. Butter's on the top floor for chicory coffee and lemon cookies.

The girl, in her favorite gray skirt, skipped down the hall and up two flights to Mr. Butter's room, ROOM 513 it said in tiny gold numbers, and at once Emily saw there was trouble. The old man's door was unlocked, partway ajar, and when she pushed it open and crept inside, she saw that bandits or gypsies had wrecked his room completely. The room, painted light green, was turned upside down: the old wooden bureau drawers were open; plates and silverware were on the floor; a dress army suit and fatigues were spread everywhere; letters, hundred and hundreds of letters, flapped about noiselessly atop the table, which was also stacked with several black military-issue dress shoes, all the same color, the same size, and yet there had to be nearly thirty of them, all at attention, a pyramid of leather soles and laces, startling in their sameness.

"Butter?" she called out, which was how she had been instructed to refer to him, told again and again to omit the proper "Mr." because of his numerous years of military service and the sense of comfort and community he had found in the American army, a fond memory of which struck him each time he was shouted for by last name only.

"Butter?" Again there was no reply.

"Butter, the birds have gone crazy," she whispered. "They're about to peck out their own eyes."

Then, from around the shaded green corner of the bedroom, Mr. Butter crawled on his hands and knees like a ninny, in a pair of faded blue pajama bottoms and a white T-shirt, the sleeves rolled, which showed the heavy blue eagle tattoo on his right bicep and the magical words IN GOD WE TRUST. They had become blotchy and almost indecipherable with age, a souvenir of his tour of the Pacific, he claimed.

"Butter, the birds haven't been fed. Where have you been anyway?" she asked.

Mr. Butter shook his head, then stopped moving. Slowly he turned and lifted his left hand to the left side of his face.

"My eye patch," he whispered. "I can't find the durn thing anywhere. For three days. I've been looking for almost three days."

Emily blinked and saw that the black eye patch he wore over his left eye was indeed missing. She screwed her head about the room, suddenly realizing why the place was such a shambles. "Well, why didn't you tell anyone?" Emily asked.

"I'm on my own here, pudding," he whispered. "Who am I gonna tell?"

"But why don't you go out and get a new one?"

Mr. Butter sat up and leaned his back against the wall. "That's like admitting you're crazy. I know it's in this house somewhere. Besides"—he rubbed the spot where his eye patch usually hung; it was pale white like the part of your shoulders the sun never seems to reach—"I need to take a bus to find one, and I don't like the idea of upsetting anyone. People'd look at me and consider me a menace like this."

"You've never cared about that before," she said.

The old man coughed and looked away. "I'm scared, I guess."

"Scared? Of what, Butter?"

"I don't know what," he whispered. "I'm scared someone's gonna shout at me."

"Shout at you?"

"I . . . I just don't know where I left the durned thing. I'm getting too old. I think I forgot to switch on my brain."

Emily pinched her lips together and did a little two-step in place.

"I might go for you, Butter. I could go and find one for you."

"Your mother wouldn't mind you riding the bus all alone?"

"I take the bus to school and back."

"That's different. It's to the same place every day."

"I know how to ride the bus, Butter."

"Well, if you're going, there's money in the honey bear," he grumbled, then closed his good eye, shaking his head. His face became slouched and gray, perhaps admitting defeat. Emily skipped over to the card table, lifted the head off the ceramic brown bear busy digging his black paws into a nest of honey, found three bills inside, and slipped the money in the waist of her gray skirt, as her friend Gert had taught her to hide mash notes and candy.

"Now don't buy me nothing made overseas," he shouted. "Or in New York City."

Emily curtsied and bolted from the room, down the front stairs, toward the steamy summertime street. Immediately, as she ran, she imagined she was not an eleven-year-old girl but a nurse during the war on a very important mission of mercy, and then not a nurse at all but a doctor whose patient was a very sick baby, running a fever perhaps, and then not a doctor but the baby's mother; it was her baby who was sick, and she was too poor to afford a doctor and had only this small amount to spend to save her precious child, the child of a man who was shot down over the Pacific on a mission of mercy, delivering medicine to natives perhaps, and this poor sick child was all that was left of a man who had been so kind and so brilliant and so charming, a naval officer and a scientist and a surgeon, and also a fresco painter, but not a boy like Dusty Evans (even though he was growing tall now and more handsome, with eyes like a grown man, and looking older each day). Then Emily realized she could play the "if" game: if she could find the eye patch for Mr. Butter by the time her mother returned home and not get caught for riding the bus alone, and if she could find the right kind of eye patch, one not made overseas or in New York City, and if she was not abducted by pirates, madmen, or gypsies, then she would truly be an adult now, and not only old enough to ride public transportation unescorted, alone, like most kids her age, but also old enough to have a baby of her own, which she had been thinking about a lot since summer had begun. She had even come up with a list of at least fifty-two names and had held the piece of stationery with the names just over her belly each night in bed for a month, hoping—and now, now she would know if she was truly ready.

2

The only patches Emily could find at Lowry's Five-and-Dime were the wrong kind. One was a great white cotton patch that nearly covered the wearer's entire profile, designed for a burn victim maybe. Another was too small, meant for a child, with a purple dinosaur painted in the center and a great white cartoon bubble that read I'M A PATCH-O-SAURUS.

"None of these will do," Emily said, shaking her head, trying purposely to sound like an adult as Mrs. Wannamaker slid the last patch back into the glass display case.

"Is it for a play you're putting on?" Mrs. Wannamaker asked. "*The Pirates and Sinbad*? Your mother could make you one from felt perhaps."

"It is certainly not for a play. It is for my dear friend who has lost his eye," Emily snapped back. "He has asked me to single-handedly save him in this most dire time."

"You might try the magic shop then, hon. They have costumes and everything. They might have a fancier-looking patch."

Emily nodded and curtsied for no reason, then folded the three dollars back within the waist of her skirt. She skipped down Elm toward the Magic Show.

3

Within moments of browsing inside the magic shop, which was silvery and blue and full of capes and canes and plastic masks, Emily found the right one: a soft black leather patch almost identical to Mr. Butter's. Just as she was about to call for the clerk, she noticed a display of invisible ink pens, but she stopped herself from checking their price. She pointed at the eye patch and nodded, placing her money in the young man's hand. The boy was thirteen or fourteen, definitely in high school, and wore a puzzled expression that seemed to say he was very amused to help Emily. As she placed the money in his hand, the boy did something strange. From the corner of his mouth he blew his hair from his eyes and smiled, and at once Emily felt a shock like static electricity run down the whole of her body. Suddenly she remembered what she had intended to forget; here it was on her dirty mind all over again.

On the last day of sixth grade, Hal Minton had passed a large science book across the back of the homeroom, from the far corner where he had been put for being "obtrusive," as Ms. Lane put it, to tall Dusty Evans, who sat on the other side of Emily. It was an eighth-grade science book that Hal had taken from his older brother, Walt Minton, who in the middle of his algebra class last year decided he did not belong in grammar school, shouted, "I am going to be the greatest strikeout pitcher any of you have ever seen," picked up his books, and strolled out the door. Walt Minton was now the head soda jerk at Russel's on Elm and maintained a high average of five chocolate malts an hour on Saturdays.

The science book didn't look any different from any other science book Emily had ever seen. It was heavy and dull green, and a page in the back had been dog-eared. Dusty Evans had pointed to it and laughed before passing the book back, and Emily, well, being the kind of sensitive dear heart that she was and sure that every joke was somehow a joke on her in some way, flipped to the dog-eared page, saw the bright pink and black and blue diagram, dropped the book from her lap like hot lava, and let out an ear-piercing scream.

The diagram in question was a picture that had kept Emily up at night: a woman, drawn in pink and blue and black, with a very normal-looking head, almost like Ms. Haskins at the grocery store, except that Ms. Haskins was a blond and not a brunette, but with the same expression, which was cheery and somewhat sleepy. There was the normal, smiling face atop a body that had been turned inside out, with the heart and stomach and curlicue veins and tendons all showing, the kind of drawing she had seen dozens of times before in her own seventh-grade science book and on the walls of museums and even on the television once when a doctor was trying to explain epilepsy. But for some reason the artist here had gone completely mad and as a joke or by mistake had inked a small pink child right inside the drawn woman's belly, as if the poor thing had been eaten, swallowed whole, entirely. When Emily glanced up at the text on the page and saw the words "Reproduction in the Human Female," the book suddenly turned into a ball of red-hot flame and pitched itself at her feet. It was as if somehow a great magical switch had been thrown and a radio program that had been playing in her head all along, although perhaps she never heard it, became so clear that it was now deafening, and the milk and crackers she had eaten for lunch suddenly began to tremble to accommodate the space needed for a great pink imaginary baby. At once she was aware that it would be her at some future date; she'd have a small person riding along inside her belly, though she had no idea how, really, or why no one had told her this before or what kind of joke she was now part of. Dusty was smiling at her from across the aisle, grinning his wicked, awful grin, and for all that, well, for all that her lungs had not stopped ringing.

4

On the bus ride home, proud of herself, for it was only two o'clock and her mother would not be home for an hour yet, and proud of herself for not spending the change on something else, such as an invisible ink pen set, the way some child might, Emily decided to wear the eye patch, slipping it over her left eye and then her right, then back to her left as she had seen Mr. Butter wear it. As she rode, she spied the other people around her with her right eye, some engaged in conversation, some reading their newspapers or magazines, some uninterested, some sleeping. There were many kinds of people on the bus—an old man in a brown hat, a boy with a blue lollipop, and a mother holding her pink-bundled baby, who began to cry, a high-pitched and scratchy cry, and the people on the bus turned to ooh and aah and smile at the poor thing. What a royal pain in the neck! Emily thought. She decided she would throw out the list of names when she got home. For now, sure to get people to notice her, Emily began to cough the way she imagined someone with consumption or whooping fever might, getting her whole body into it, flailing her arms about, until a kind woman behind her in a white scarf leaned over the seats, held Emily's shoulders, patted her back, and whispered, "My poor dear, my poor dear," at which Emily nodded and ended her fit thankfully. "Must you ride the bus all alone, my dear?" the woman asked and offered her a piece of hard butterscotch candy.

"My father was shot down over the Pacific, and my mother, well, she is a gypsy. We are very poor. I have been sent to get her medicine."

"You poor thing," the woman exclaimed, patting Emily's back again. "And your eye? Your poor eye. Were you born . . . like this?"

"Oh, no, that was for my brother. He had no eyes, so I donated one to him," Emily whispered, holding the patch to her face as she began to enact a very believable coughing fit once again.

IN THE ARMS OF SOMEONE YOU LOVE

In Cuba there are many has-been magicians.

It is not a nice feeling to lose your wife to one of them, you can believe me. But in times of war, when magic and mesmerism are held as a kind of science, like mathematics and firearms and astronomy, a kind of high art, really, there are many fine young men of our generation who take to performing in the music halls and vaudeville theaters and cocktail lounges, places where a clerk in the Bureau of Calculations can take his beautiful mute wife for a nice night out on an honest man's pay. I'm not a funny man, I have to admit that. I have a sense of humor, but there's nothing about me that I'd call funny. I am an observer. I notice things. How the hem of my wife's dress is sewn up with nothing more than all the heft and weight of my oldest desires from when I was a boy and did not understand what love was and what occurs between a woman and a man. Yes, I notice things. Her long black hair was a kind of esplanade to the fountain of her almond-shaped face. Most light gently faded whenever she closed her eyes, and the daybreak was our time alone and only ours. Her bare shoulders, in their own way, had a certain way of defining a certain time of a certain kind of night. And her smile, oh, her smile was an instrument to define all kinds of times of day.

As I said, I took my wife out one night during a dangerous time, when the revolutionary forces were closing in on the capital and our president was busy packing his things, sweating, murmuring, "*Ahora, ahora, ahora estoy muerto.*" I took her out because I could not watch her another night as we sat close beside the radio, her soft black eyebrows knitted in a way that created a deadly serious sheet of doom on her face.

"Tonight, my friends, tonight," said the host, who wore a red cummerbund and had a very angelic expression for an eighty-year-old man. He tapped the silver microphone once and then said, "Tonight I present to you a very dear friend of mine, Gilberto, all the way from Spain."

Spanish refugees who were stranded on our island from their own revolution showed their camaraderie and disdain by slowly stirring their drinks at the bar all the way in the back and nodding silently.

"Gilberto!"

The man took the stage, and right away I felt my life come unraveled. Quickly. Painlessly. Only twice in my life have I ever felt like that. The first time I was five, and my mother went at my father with a butcher's knife. He knocked it from her hand, and then they began kissing and lovemaking frantically. Love was something my parents were proud to have us see; our family being so poor and living in such an impoverished community, it was one thing the government, the pope, the Federalists, or the student revolutionaries could not take away. The second time, as I've said, it became clear to me that I was doomed as soon as Gilberto took the stage. It felt as if all the buttons on my tuxedo shirt had come undone. It was as if I hadn't spent most of my salary repairing the seams in my jacket and having my shoes shined and my mustache clipped. It was as if I was not wearing the red Bureau of Calculations pin on my lapel and had never gotten my degree and had never designed the plans for the new bridge that would, of course, be given the president's name. It was as if I had disappeared completely and no one else in the world had ever existed. It was quite obvious before I even looked at my wife. I had lost it all, just as I had always feared, and all quite suddenly.

"For my first trick," Gilberto began, "I will need a member of the audience to assist me. A female, perhaps, eh?" When I looked at my peach, my fruit, my only permutation in a sea of insolvent calculations and gardens of insoluble dreams (I still remember what she said when I asked her to marry me: "Would you mind asking me again tomorrow or next week?" I asked, "Why! Why? Why should I ask again if you are going to mock me? I think love is something in the blood, in the heart. It requires very little thought. It is not mathematics, my Eloise." And she said, "I want to study you, *amor*. I want to be sure I will be strong enough." "For what?" I asked. "I want to be sure I will be able to carry a baby who will most definitely be born looking just like you, with such a thoughtful head on his shoulders, such steady arms and dependable lips and sturdy legs, such a large and beautiful hero's face . . . "), well, right then, thoughts of marriage aside and years and years of connubial bliss, I could tell everything was about to change. Gilberto, in a smashing black tuxedo and with the most sensitively drawn black mustache and eyes—oh Lord, eyes that could confound and belittle and bewitch. He was tall and had an enormous forehead; you could easily imagine beautiful women running their fingers all along it. This man, an international traveler, a celebrity, a guest of our sad nation, could have any woman he desired and fly her off with him to some other sad little island. And just then the spotlight was in my face, and he was taking my bride, my tulip, my wife, my Eloise, this half-American girl who was born the daughter of an ambassador and a downstairs maid and who wore the pride and disgrace of both her parents on each of her splendidly red lips, a girl not born mute but who lost her voice one day when she saw our poor baby, Graciella, get hit by a government bus full of convicts being transferred from the prison to the death house. The accident took place right in front of our house, and my wife, Eloise, screamed. She screamed, but not in time, and it was as if all the things she had ever held in and all the words she would ever say were swept away alongside the huge silvery bumper that killed our daughter and made my wife silent since that long-ago summer day. I looked up at the stage, and Gilberto was taking my wife's hand and saying something like, "What a jewel, what an enchanting creature you are!" as if I was only a bundle of secondhand clothes sitting there, trying to keep down my drink. He said, "Let me guess. You are an American, yes?" She nodded and then shook her head, and the magician laughed and his little mustache twitched. Then he said, "A beautiful American all alone in Cuba. What can be more dangerous, more stunning?" He winked at me, and then he said, "And now, my friends, the trick! An illusion of mesmerism!" He lifted his hand and made a magical gesture, leaning all his fingers together tight, as if he was focusing every electrical spark in his body on his fingertips where they were gathering and rising and taking shape, and then he took my wife's hand in his other, nonmagical hand and said, "Sleep!" Very gently, very lovingly, he touched his dangerous fingers to my wife's lips, and then, just like that, she was asleep and swooning in his arms. He caught her like an old pro, this one, and I was on my feet, enraged, and my wife was wearing a smile I had never, ever seen, and the thought occurred to me that I am an unlucky man in the way that I am lucky to have a favorable post and a decent apartment and all my fingers and toes and a beautifully mute wife, but all of it is always just about to slip from my hands, day or night, night or day. I am in a constant state of waiting for everything to fall apart around me, and now it had happened. Just then I realized this was not a trick at all, this was no kind of magic; people were clapping, and my wife was recovering. But I had seen it, I had seen something. They had been duped; they had all been duped. He was not using magic, he was simply doing what all great lovers know how to do. He was using the lips, the lips that were the garden passageway to the soul; it was not mesmerism at all but a sign that this man, this magician, had designs on my wife. People were still clapping and then there was a silence, which was not a silence but a scream that had happened many miles away; it had just made it to our ears in the form of a whisper, which made everyone quiet at the same time because it was the kind of sound that happened on the inside of your ears, and slowly, very slowly, you knew what it was. The doors crashed in, and Manuel, the cigarette merchant from down the street, fell to the ground and then lifted his head and shouted, "The rebels have taken the capital!" right before his eyes closed for the last time and all his words turned red. Then there was a kind of panic I had never seen in civilized humanity. Ladies were fighting over each other's mink stoles, trying for the door; men of noble careers were stealing expensive cigars from the upset silver trays; a low-ranking government official who had paid a waitress for a look at her ankles was kissing her bare shins, saying, "I will be killed next. I will be killed next, and this is all I wanted out of life, to be near a beautiful woman and kiss her feet every night." There was an explosion down the street, and I realized there was nowhere to run to, there was nowhere to run. My Eloise was at my side and trying to smile, and I looked at her and thought, Well, at least my bride and I will make it out of here alive. We were on the street, which was black and overrun with people, and there was a fire at the post office down the road. Students from the university were throwing furniture into the fire and shouting and clapping their hands, and just then Señor Lunes from my office ran up to me and said, "Señor Hidalgo, we have been marked. They are killing all scientists and all government men, and we are both, we are both, my friend, we are both." I said, "You are being much too dramatic, old Lunes." He smiled at me and shook his head and walked away, and just then I noticed there was a huge bullet hole in the side of his skull, right above his ear. My friend Lunes was already dead and walking around because he hadn't said his good-byes properly or kissed his wife yet, and somehow I knew, I knew that I, too, was already dead. I just hadn't been shot yet. So right then I started calculating how soon it would be before the rebels would enter our barrio and find me standing there, hopeless. And suddenly I remembered a dream of a memory I once had. I was a boy, a very young boy, and I was standing on the beach. It was very early in the morning, and there were people hunting crabs and a man, drunk, sleeping on the white sand. I stood there on that beach and felt like a hero suddenly because it occurred to me I could stare directly into the sun and still see—and not just see, I could see everything: my family and neighborhood and my birth and my death and the whole life that was still ahead of me. It seemed even then I knew I was a hero because I could see the outcome of everything, the sum total, the remainder, the indivisible final graph, and even then I could know that my whole life depended on this exact strange moment, this impossible mathematical conclusion, this calculation of future and past. I turned to my wife and kissed her lips and then grabbed hold of the great Gilberto by his silky tuxedo coat. He had been standing nearby smoking a long cigarette very elegantly. I said to him, "If you are capable of love, take this one with you and get out of Havana as fast as you can." The great Gilberto nodded and took my wife's hand, and Eloise became frantic, digging her nails into my neck to keep from leaving. I looked at Gilberto and he looked at me, and just then a volley of machine-gun bullets flew like molten sparrows right over my head. Voices were shouting, "Kill the men who forsake our Jesus for the gods of hypocrisy and science!" I gave Gilberto an imploring look, and somehow he could understand; just like that he did his trick again and touched the electrical fingers to the lips, the soft petals of flesh that were mine and would not ever give a single word of discomfort or carelessness. She folded into his arms, and I watched them go; and just then I thought how funny it was that I should die in a tuxedo and how strange it was that I had had my jacket fixed for this occasion and what trouble I would be saving the local mortician when he laid me down to rest. Gilberto and my wife were now a soft black dot in the sheltered glow of the leaning streetlights, and I thought, Yes, my friend, someday soon you, too, will die. I thought this magician would die one day, maybe after a long time, maybe after many years of loving my wife, and she would always be my wife, in heaven or with the saints who took to fooling with angels and were cast down to hell in disgrace. She would always be mine, and time could only make him more fond of her, and when he died, he would be alone in the end—and not only alone, but without her. It occurred to me that in a way I was him, this magician, living out his death, and he was me living out my life with her because he could save her and I could not, and it was only a matter of time, after all, before we would all die. It would be as if this devil's barter had never been made, and the guns would stop firing and the students would be quiet and concern themselves with liberty instead of freedom, and all the busts of famous men that had been broken would be mended, and everything that had been overturned would be put back in its place. It occurred to me, my tulip, that love and countrymen are strange this way, and my neck and ear were bleeding now—and, yes, my tulip, love and countrymen are just this strange.

FLASH ITEM! LAMUE LOSES IN FINAL ROUND!

Contender Folds after Knockout!

WALLACE, Kan.—Buddy Lamue, previously unsuccessful two-time challenger to the ILCO Insurance Midwest Boxing Association Welterweight Championship, fell in love again last Saturday afternoon. He had just started working for Double Deuce Collections and Repossessions and went to drop off a large amount of cash at his boss's house when he met Mrs. Donna Dover for the first time. "In a black bathing suit, she could have been some starlet's stand-in maybe," Lamue remarked later.

After a series of highballs mixed at Mrs. Donna Dover's request, former boxer Buddy became nervous, remarking, "Where is Mr. Dover?" and "Maybe I should leave." Mrs. Dover ignored his apparent discomfort, preferring instead to stare at him silently. Taken by her long blond hair, Hollywood good looks, and blue bedroom eyes, Buddy Lamue invited Mrs. Dover to view something "so beautiful it'll make you wonder" in the trunk of one of the cars he had repossessed that afternoon. Following Buddy Lamue to a 1972 yellow Mercury Cougar parked out front, Mrs. Donna Dover became quiet. Buddy Lamue only smiled as he found the right key and unlocked the trunk of the automobile. Inside the silver trunk were three dozen small pink ballerina slippers, obviously intended for children. "They're so pretty and tiny, I feel dumb just looking at them," Buddy Lamue stated. Mrs. Dover stared at Buddy Lamue for "a very long time." Then Buddy remarked, "We shouldn't," to which Mrs. Dover replied, "Say that again, and I'll eat you up," ending with Buddy Lamue's final remark: "We shouldn't."

TIJUANA WOMEN

1

Tijuana women make it hard on a man all week long. I learned this lesson from a man my mother used to date named Tony Montenegro. In the fifties, Tony Montenegro was a Mexican movie star, and he had his own white stucco ranch in Tijuana. He would drive us down there from Palm Springs, where my mother and I lived, in his big silver Olds Eighty-Eight, and the entire time the man did not stop smoking. The sand-dusted highway was one continuous cigarette to him, and I imagined the stubs trailing behind us back to where my real father was lying in a hospital bed, much like small lanterns marking our path maybe. The soft cloth top would be down on Tony's car, and my mother would have her head wrapped in a silvery scarf that would be pressed against Tony's shoulder very tightly. The stars would be flashing overhead like quick stab wounds of light, and the whole time I would be thinking, It is wrong to leave him at home, no matter how far we drive.

"To begin our Spanish lesson—in Tijuana, Monday is called *lunes,* which means day of the moon," Tony says. This makes me think. The sound of Monday is the exact opposite of the sound of "I'll be with you soon." It is the beginning of a length of time no one I have ever known desires. It is salt on a peanut butter and jelly sandwich that your mother's boyfriend does not know how to make. It summons the worst qualities of having to wait. Monday is an unlucky day in any language, I think. I will spend the first part of my summer vacation on Tony's ranch, because my own father will not be released from the VA hospital for another two weeks, which means at least another few days of watching colts being broken from the window in the kitchen and being told to go in the other room and listen to the radio. This is until I walk in on Tony unsnapping my mother's garters with his feet and he gives me an old six-chambered pistol and tells me to go play out back. For a moment the gun is so heavy in my hand that the sting of anger on my face is not enough to stop me.

I tell one of the ranch hands that Tony demands bullets for the gun he has given me. The ranch hand has a blue neckerchief and silver spurs. He looks at me funny, then nods and gives me a small paper box full of rounds. I fit them in the small silver tubes and leave the paper box by the old tree with an ax stuck in the center of it, the tree which over years and years has grown around the tool so that the wooden handle looks just like a branch. I climb the low hills, past the fence, to the dark gray shacks out back. I see a row of tall thin cylinders made of glass and immediately begin to shoot at these. They are novena candles. A man with a soft gray beard comes running out from one of the shacks, hollering. He is cursing me, I think. He sees the gun, sees who I am, a white child, and shakes his head, knowing I have come from the Montenegro ranch. "You a bad boy," he says and then shakes his finger at me. "You make evil." I back away carefully down the hill and run along the dusty valley, aiming the gun at everything. Only later, when I find a dead dog lying on its side in some weeds, do I understand what the bearded man means. Somehow I think I have killed the dog by shooting out the candles, and I cannot let go of the feeling of guilt.

4

My mother buys a blond wig to look more glamorous, she says. Tony takes us to a restaurant in town to celebrate. The whole time I know what the wig is for. It is to keep her from being recognized. My father, Lou, is in a VA hospital carving her name in the metal frame of his bed. He carves it over and over again, transmitting it like a message. Other sailors and dogfaces pick it up on some frequency that I imagine all military men share and give my mother disapproving looks when Tony wraps his arm around her neck. I imagine one of the sailors exploding from the table, stabbing Tony with a steak knife, then saying, "Semper fi! That was for you wherever you are, Lou!" But we eat at the fancy restaurant without event. We walk around town. We go home to bed. I am tucked in early. I imagine the wig crawling about the house at night, contemptuous and proud, as I try to get to sleep. Outside I hear the horses neigh and, in the distance, wild dogs barking. I imagine my father, Lou, searching for us, showing a picture of my mother and me to everyone he meets on the street, pedaling in a silver wheelchair through the dark of town. People see my photo and recognize me—"*Sí, sí*"—but then look at my mother with her natural brown hair, and no one can agree. So my father pulls himself along, the wheels of his chair spinning gently around. I decide then I must get rid of the wig if I am to help my father out.

5

Tony gets a tattoo of my mother's name on his chest the next day. He tears open his blue-flowered shirt, and my mother screams with pleasure. They begin to kiss, using all of their lips. I use this diversion to slip into my mother's room, take the wig, hide it under my shirt, and follow the wooden fence posts down to the small dust brown canyon. I take the wig out from under my shirt and bury it under the brush, then follow the dry brown weeds to where I had seen the dead dog days before. When I get all the way down the valley, a small Mexican girl with her hair in braids is kneeling beside the dead dog, petting its side very softly.

"*Es mío,*" she says, and I only stand there, afraid to look at the dog anymore.

When I get back to the ranch, my mother and Tony are having lunch. My mother stops me and kisses me on my cheek.

"I guess someone did not like my wig," my mother says, and Tony is silent, glaring at me.

"Mexican boys would not behave like that," he says, crossing his fork and his knife to let the maids know he is done. I go back outside and find some full bottles of beer to shoot at, and they explode like old castles in the midday sun.

6

"The wig was expensive," Tony says that night at dinner.

"It's no matter," my mother says.

"It's no matter to you maybe."

"He is a boy. He doesn't understand," my mother says.

"He does not understand stealing?" Tony says back.

"Please, do not mention it anymore."

"Aye," he mumbles, kissing my mother's neck. "Tijuana women make it hard on a man all week. No rest even on Sunday, eh?" From the kitchen I hear him say this and don't know what he means, but I like it for some reason. "You are a Tijuana woman now, eh?" Tony asks, and my mother says nothing, only coos.

7

The tiger tattoo is the one I admire. It is a very narrow, powerful looking tiger that stretches across your entire arm, and its claws draw inky blood from your skin. We go into town the next day so Tony can get a heart drawn around my mother's name. As we are watching Tony being tattooed, I look outside and see a young girl walking down the street, wearing my mother's blond wig. She is small and proud, and her few friends treat her like she is a queen. They all walk together in a procession behind the girl with the wig, which is lit up by the sun. It is so beautiful, I can't say a word about it. I just sit and stare.

I don't mention any part of what happened in Mexico later on. It is all part of the same secret to me, I think. There are some things that might make me angry, some things that are very wrong, and some things that are only for me— things that are very beautiful, full of beauty, like the old pistol and the tiger tattoo and the girl with the wig lit up by the sun. They are moments I refuse to share. They are moments I have never told anyone.

HOLD ON TO YOUR HAT

A very strange thing happened to our old friend Charlie as he crossed the street: a chrome-lined city bus roared past with a plume of soft white exhaust, and the snow that had been persistent the last few days slowly began to desist. White petals of it still gently made their way to melt on the sidewalk, quietly, and the shiny traffic lights flashed from innocent green to dull yellow and then red, red as a kind of warning. And just as Charlie was climbing up the hefty curb, folded newspaper in hand, his brand-new gray felt hat flew from the top of his head, and as he reached into the air for it, he felt himself being lifted, completely, from his heavy, earthbound feet.

In one short moment he was in the air, dangling like a foreign gray flag, hanging on to the hat with the very ends of the fingertips of his right hand. He was rising, rising up, the fragile bling and din and honk of the traffic fading below him, his shiny brown shoes sweeping hopelessly about the cloudy air for some kind of footing. And yet, as Charlie's suit coat billowed like a dinghy's sail and a small but polite traffic cop, decked out completely in blue, lifted his finger and pointed, making his mustached mouth into a small O of surprise and wonder, Charlie only closed his eyes and thought, Why? Why, too, was this happening?

The big bluster of a hemlock wedding had been called off, and only days before at that. Priscilla, dainty as ever in her haunted white wedding gown, simply dropped her face into her hands and began to cry inconsolably, her mother patting her back and whispering right away, "There will be others, surely, but this dress . . . this dress is timeless, dear." Priscilla, her cruel blond curls done up high on her head like a kind of elegant French pastry, nodded and, despite her grief, whispered, "I am going to be an old maid all because of him!" She pointed, her striking features now so sharp they could cut glass or surely the outer edges of someone's heart, to which Charlie, in his usual cowardly way, shook his head and slowly crept out, holding his hand over his chest in the pose of the guilty man.

One day prior to that moment, the moment of his ending the most dubious engagement we had ever been party to—because, let's face it, Priscilla was a banshee, a real tart-mouthed, low-down, social-climbing banshee, and how long had he actually planned on being married to her in the first place?—our old friend Charlie had sat on the rough blue paper of the very sterile examining room table, his backside bare and cold against the changing sheet, his legs like they were now, at this moment of height and airlessness, dangling, sweeping back and forth nervously. When Dr. DeValle strode in, head down, glasses like a shield over the crypts of his blue eyes, he only glanced at Charlie's papers and then looked up and drew in a breath. There, right there, as the old man breathed, stern in his white doctor's coat, soft brown age spots glistening on his forehead like tiny infinite suns, the suns of days that had passed and the suns of days yet to come, Charlie felt his breath go, too, without his control, a reflex of very real terror, his hands cramping along the paper. Dr. DeValle began to speak, cleared his throat, and finally, finally, wordlessly, shook his head. No, no, Charlie thought. He is shaking his head, so it means no. No means negative, and that is good. Negative is good. No is good. Then Charlie realized what the man was telling him: it was, *No, no, I do not know how to tell you this. No, I do not want to tell you this, but . . . but . . .*

Without a sound, Charlie's fate was sealed, and like his awful fiancée, Priscilla, he began to cry. He would lie to Priscilla only a day later, saying, "I cannot marry you." Which may have been true enough but withheld: *Somehow I have developed cancer of the colon, and I did not see or hear it happening. I was too embarrassed, too embarrassed to ask anyone until it was too late, and now in this act, my one act of braveness and charity, my one act of love, which may be the only true act of love I have ever committed to, for, or against you, because I do not love you, and I am too afraid to admit this, in truth, in honesty, but now I am telling you this once and for all: I cannot and will not marry you because I am giving up. I am giving up and am at my end and have accepted this gratefully.*

Why, too, then, he thought as he stared down at the city growing smaller below, headlights from the automobiles crisscrossing like a luminescent spiderweb, why, after all that, was this happening? A woman, wearing a black dress and applying lipstick to her lips, glanced out her office building window and, seeing Charlie, still grasping tightly to the felt hat with the fingers of his right hand, dropped the lipstick from her mouth and let out a scream, shaking the glass in the pane. Charlie continued rising higher, no longer afraid so much as curious, his feet no longer kicking about, and like a large gray kite, he continued drifting upward, the sounds of traffic, honking horns and taxicabs swerving from their stands, bellboys calling out, and whistles and sirens and bells all disappearing, except for the Salvation Army choir that was working its magic on a corner, the coronet player playing louder than the rest his rendition of "O Little Town of Bethlehem," the sound of it, far and cheery, like a whisper underwater. And Charlie smiled suddenly, remembering the game he played with little Mary Alice at the lake when he was nine years old. Holding hands, the two of them would hold their breath and swim underwater and then shout words to each other, giggling bubbles and trying to guess what the other had said. "I love you . . . I love you," he had tried to say, but she had only heard, "Gazoo, gazoo." They would repeat this to each other and laugh about it, even years later at a café with Mary Alice's second fiancé, and only Charlie knew what he had meant and would mean until something miraculous swept him over into death.

By now he was somewhere above most of the skyscrapers, office buildings, and apartment houses, and he was smiling, no longer frightened but amazed, his heart beating wildly like a sailor in love. He had both hands on his hat now, and the city was only a sketch, a very soft gray charcoal work that at this height had turned completely into smoke, and just as he caught sight of a daring flock of pigeons, practicing their triangular maneuvers, building magnificent figure eights in the air, then another, then another, Charlie remembered the big red balloon he had been given as a child and had—in a moment of what? mischievousness? curiosity? childish wonderment?—shoved the birthday gift out the apartment window. He let the balloon go, watching it rise, rise, rise, until his grandfather, in a shiny blue paper party hat that was attached tightly with elastic about his narrow face, clapped his hand on the boy's shoulder. Instead of offering anger or disappointment, his grandfather smiled and said, "You're a very smart boy, Charlie. You knew exactly what to do with it," and Charlie, unsure what to say, only nodded, and Charlie's mother, seeing the balloon drift lazily upward like a happy drunk, scolded her boy, saying, "No more balloons for you." Years later, many years later, in school, Charlie learned about air pressure and physics and what happened as objects approached the very upper levels of what scientists and boring, gray-bearded nuns referred to as "our atmosphere," and suddenly, remembering all this, Charlie began to panic and was overcome with sweat and chills, knowing that if he continued to ascend at this rate, something—his heart, his stomach, the cancer in the southernmost region of his large colon—would explode and, hat or not, he would be nothing but red vapor very, very quickly.

But he did not continue to rise. Leveling off then, just above the faintest reaches of the tallest of the tall skyscrapers, he floated into a kind of airstream, some kind of current, and like a great, wide, invisible hand, it gently pushed him eastbound, and there, below, the city and its river and, farther out, the shiny blue jewel of water that marked the borders of the metropolis grew like a great moving sheet, flecked with ribbons of light. Charlie had the feeling he would blow out to sea and then that would be that, and yet, instead, he was blown back in the opposite direction, then switched again, and here, too, he thought he would find his fate, trapped, in limbo then, blown about back and forth over a city he would never see clearly again. He thought of all his favorite places: his bed with the blue country blanket Priscilla had given him that reminded him of his childhood room; the back table at Garamoundt, shady, at which he had traded kisses with a waitress when he had only just turned twenty; a fort he had built in the woods by his uncle's house when he was twelve, constructed out of old tires and fallen limbs, now gone, gone, all of it gone—along with his favorite people, like Billy Dobbs, the fellow across the cubicle from him who had a small scar along his chin and always had a dirty joke or some limerick to spare; and Bud the doorman, portly, clever, who always whistled "Charge!" whenever Charlie came in; or Miss Adams, Miss Adams, Miss Adams, the blue-eyed secretary who brought powdered doughnuts every Friday and seemed too sweet, too youthful, too darling to ever ask out for drinks. She had worn a Santa hat of red velvet with white fur trim at the Christmas party last year, and while the others were decorating the office Christmas tree, Miss Adams had sat demurely on Charlie's desk, so small, her red skirt rising above her knees, revealing the most darling, really, the most gorgeous ankles he had ever seen, and she had held a small piece of green mistletoe over her head, and every part of his body, every small muscle, every weak organ, every human tissue in him had ached, ached to lean in, just lean in and take the plunge, kiss her so strongly, so deeply that he would die against her lap right there, like a fireworks display going up in a cloud of panic and smoke. But he didn't, he didn't; he blushed and raised his left hand, showing the shiny platinum engagement band Priscilla had picked out for him, and Miss Adams went red in the face, dropping the mistletoe to their feet.

It was then, at that moment, that one right there, when Miss Adams's wide blue eyes went gray and she shrugged her shoulders, apologizing profusely, almost crying out of embarrassment. "What kind of girl do you think I must be?" she was asking, shaking her head, and he was thinking, Lovely, lovely, just lovely. And she pulled off her Santa cap and skittered down the blue carpeting between the rows and rows of cubicles, and Charlie stood there and pulled off his wedding band and started to speak up, started to shout to her, "No, please, please come back. Please come back," knowing it was the right thing, the only thing to save him now, the coward, the yellow-bellied, lily-livered coward. But just then the telephone at his desk began to ring, and somehow, from the desperate, shrill tone, he knew who it was almost immediately: Priscilla, oh, Priscilla.

Even at this height he could hear that phone ringing, ringing, ringing, again and again, and now, far up and above, floating all alone over the populace in the solitude of evening, he saw himself a year ago, in the office, mistletoe at his feet. He saw himself slide the ring back along his finger, defeated. You coward, you fool, you dolt. He had been too afraid, too weak, too unwilling. He had been done in a year ago in that moment, just then, and he hadn't ever seen it. But he saw it now. He saw it now. Charlie was descending at that moment, not too quickly, the hat filling with air as the shapes of automobiles and traffic lights and street signs became more and more clear, shining, precious, bright.

Now the gray brim of the hat wavered against the rush of it all, and all he could think was, Miss Adams, Miss Adams. I will take a taxi back to the office and find her there and kiss the tip of her nose as quick as I can, because, after all, life is only a series of strange turns—what strange turns, what strange turns. Again he was descending, descending, the pavement black and slick with melted snow, and his brown shoes were moving on it now, quicker, quicker, and very soon he was skipping inside the golden elevator of the Skyway Building, and Miss Adams—Laura, Laura was her first name—was at her desk and looking up.

Well, everything was just old news after that.

I'LL BE YOUR SAILOR

1

We would go there to cheat, more lonely than pirates with knives in their teeth. At the time, Hannah was a waitress at Ahoy There, Mateys! this seafood restaurant with a seafaring theme, and she would be wearing the whole getup: black eye patch, black britches, white puffy blouse, red neckerchief. In a flash she would be a different person and bare in my arms, and we would be kissing. We would meet in the laundry room in the basement of the apartment building and do what we went there to do without hardly ever speaking. Hannah did not like to talk to me or anybody. We would kiss until the washing machine began singing, buzzing loudly that it had finished its rinse cycle, and when it did, it meant it was time for Hannah to leave—even if we were in the middle of what other people might call adultery. Sometimes, sometimes, I would just have to say something. "Hannah," I'd say sometimes, "I've had enough of this. We are adults. We should not have to sneak around like this. We should not have to hide our lives. I think you should leave him. I think we should get married."

"I'm already married," she'd say. The laundry room would smell like a month of summer that only scientists could ever have invented, like Dew Soft or Bunny Fluffy or Rainstorm Clean, and we would be pressed up close against the dryer. She would pinch my nose and begin laughing. "I'm already married, and I refuse to commit bigamy."

"Bigamy? You're married to the wrong guy," I'd say.

"Who says you're the right guy?" she'd say.

"I say," I'd tell her. "I'm saying I'm the right guy."

"I need to get back up there. Bob is watching TV," she'd whisper and smack a kiss on my cheek. She'd put on her pink robe and pat down her red hair. She'd still be barefoot and itching the back of her leg with the front of her other foot. Along her neck there would be tiny marks from my whiskers, lighter red than her darling freckles.

"So is that a yes or a no?" I'd ask.

"It is a nice way of not answering," she'd say and give me a playful shove, then disappear behind the laundry room door and bounce up the stairs with small happy thuds. I'd lay my face against the washer and feel the vibrations against my chin and think, What can you do to prove you love somebody when love is the reason she's been so unhappy? But I could never think of an answer. I'd watch her pirate uniform through the round window of the washing machine, like me, like my heart, gently drowning.

2

A bad haircut got me this big cash settlement, so I didn't have to work for a while. You know how it happens, I guess. I received a coupon in the mail for a free haircut and went down to one of those conglomerate haircutting places in the mall. The lovely young hairstylist at the Super Haircut must have been at the end of her rope; from the blank impression of her black eyes, it looked as if she had been trying to kill herself slowly with tranquilizers, though maybe I'm just speculating. I commented about how nice it was, her taking the time to wash my hair. Well, it was nice, because to be honest, I had not been touched by another human being in months, and my heart was weaker than a baby bird's, and the stylist must have decided I was trying to be funny or that I looked like an old flame of hers who had done her wrong, so there was vengeance in her eyes and the scissors in her hand. The haircut she saw fit for my head must have been named Malice, and I ended up losing the only thing going for me at the time: my required corporate hairstyle. The next day I was fired. There was a new office manager at work who decided to make an example of me, and like that, I was out.

One night a few weeks later a poorly shot commercial came on with Lloyd Bennet, the "lawyer who wants to make it right!" He was lovingly fingering huge wads of brand-new cash, so much cash that it looked like the prize money from a board game. But it wasn't, it was all real, so I said, "Sign me up for some of that, Lloyd." I actually said that to him in person, and instead of being put off, he was happy that I was clear about what he did for a living. I told him how I had lost my job after this one very bad haircut, and we won our case, just like that, and I found that even though I hadn't worked in over two months, I was now rich and wearing the same very mysterious, very baby blue terry cloth bathrobe around the house, wondering from whence it came. And that was how I met Hannah the first time. She was down in the laundry room, crying, washing her uniform as she did every night to get rid of the stink of the sea, and I went down there to clean my famous blue robe and saw her crying. For no reason she just started hugging me. As you might have guessed, I fell in love with her by the end of the week.

3

To occupy the rest of my time and to avoid watching game shows on TV all day and night, ordering Chinese food, and stealing my one upstairs neighbor's racy fashion magazines with interesting article titles like "What Women Need to Know about Achieving Multiple Orgasms without a Man," I began to figure out exactly who else was living in my building with me. Why? Because, like I said, I was lonely. With my job at Banyard's Mail-Order Catalog Sales, as lousy as it was, there had been people around, people on the phone, people in the office, unhappy people, angry people, people who were complaining, but at least there were always people. And if not people, there was Banyard's Male Model Man. With his tiny clipped mustache and debonair smile, he was on the cover of every catalog and pictured on the many boxes of hair cream, boots, and flannel shirts—hundreds of him, stacked in tidy yellow boxes all around me, so that, considering everything, I never really felt lonely.

In the apartment building there were ten units. I knew no one. Faces, yes, but I had no names to go with the faces and even less of an idea about their lives. I knew there were at least two kids who lived three floors somewhere above me, a brother and a sister, because every afternoon around three I'd hear them come marching up the stairs, shoving each other and arguing. The little girl, who I think was older, always seemed to be very bossy. So one day as I heard them coming up, I stepped out into the hall and said, "Hey, why don't you stop being so bossy to your brother, kid?"

The little girl had a puffy pink jacket on, red ribbons in her brown hair, and one of those long noses that let you know early on that she was born to be a harpy. "He's not my brother," she spat. "He's my cousin."

"Well, why not be nice to him sometime?" I asked. I had to be a sight for the kids. I was in my famous blue robe, I had not shaved for many, many days, and I think perhaps I had not worn shoes in over a lifetime. As I was staring at them, I kept scratching at the Red Mysterious Itch that had begun on my elbow days before. The little girl looked up, grabbed her cousin's hand, and said, "Let's go, Junior," and I said, "Hey, we're having a conversation here. Don't you know the fundamentals of conversation?" The little girl said, "You're weird," and I said, "But rich like a miser." She pulled on the kid's hand and said, "Come on, Junior," and it was just then that I noticed the kid had a big yellow butterfly in a jar. I said, "Hey, kid, you better poke airholes in the lid for it." The poor kid hadn't, so like a hero I took out my keys from my robe pocket, took the glass jar from Junior's hand, poked some holes in the top, and that soft, earthy smell that insects have rose out. The kid, Junior, said, "Thanks, but it's already dead." I asked, "Why do you have a dead butterfly, kid?" and he said, "To look at." I watched the girl drag her cousin by his sleeve up the stairs as the boy waved good-bye to me. For some reason I decided at that moment that I had to do anything to get those kids to like me.

Like I said, Hannah was not much of a talker, and also she was a lush, a really bad drunk, but otherwise she was a really likable lady, the best lady I had ever been involved with. About a year ago she had moved into the building with her husband, who was "in the business of cleaning pools," as he said it, and who, probably like all the husbands of the world, didn't appreciate her the way she thought she should be appreciated. Go figure. So Hannah had developed this interesting pattern where she would go down to the laundry room to wash the pirate uniform every night at eleven, after her shift. Then she'd put on all the rest of the washers and dryers and sob as loud as she could and get lousy drunk. She had empty bottles of brandy hidden behind all the washing machines, like two dozen maybe. Also, she had a habit of chewing her fingernails. There were hundreds of these small red crescent-shaped fake nails lying on the floor beside the dryer and anywhere else she sat for more than five minutes. Apparently her husband, Bob, never noticed any of the signs. I don't know if I would have either. I had lived with a girl for a while and didn't notice she had slowly started hating me for using the word "excelsior" even though I did it accidentally and without malice, and I ended up saying it about five minutes before she left for good.

After we met in the laundry room that first time, Hannah began stopping by my apartment when Bob was out somewhere, someplace. Sometimes she would be drunk. We'd watch TV, soap operas she'd asked me to videotape or celebrity profiles, or we'd play some board game like Suspicion! or talk about what I had read in whatever magazine or newspaper I had stolen from my neighbor's mail that day. Then one night, in the middle of her sitting in the crummy green chair across the room, chewing her fingernails and being lit up, doing a regular crummy job of it, biting her fingertips off, and me over on the sofa working on a new bag of potato chips, she looked at me like a drunk ghost and asked, "Did you ever do anything really, really bad?" I knew exactly what she meant by it, and I shook my head. "No, no way." We ended up doing what she was talking about anyway. Fumbling into the bedroom, fumbling with each other's clothes, and when it was all over, fumbling to think of something to say. All I can add now is that she was very nice about it, very gentle at first, but she had the dirtiest mouth in bed I have heard in my life, which was okay by me. In bed she called me a filthy pimp. No woman had ever called me that before. So in the end it got to be a regular thing, her coming over and us drinking and then going into the other room to fool around. Sometimes we had these long bouts of groping with a lot going on, all kinds of kinky stuff I had never done before, all rough talk, and other times she would get into bed and just go to sleep. It didn't matter to me either way. I was just happy to be with someone, doing something, even just watching her asleep in a drunken stupor, her eyes fluttering and twitching.

5

These were the days of sunshine; these were the days when I began to hang out with my little neighbor Junior and his cousin when they came home from school. They would knock on my door when they came home or ring the buzzer or stick some secret message on a piece of notebook paper under the door, like the word "blatto." It was a word Junior had made up to describe how it felt getting hit by a bus when he was real young, the accident that had wiped out his mom and was the reason he lived with Crissy, his older cousin, and her family. As it turned out, Crissy was older, eleven, and Junior was eight. That kid, Junior, man, he cracked me up. He made up words or songs all the time. The two of them would come by, and we would all watch cartoons and pig out on snacks. Since Crissy's mom and dad worked late, it was probably better that they hung out with me anyway. We didn't tell anyone they were coming over, because I know it seems a little creepy. But like I said, I was lonely, and it gave me something to do, like a job. I would make cookies for them while they did their homework, and then we'd all play a rousing game of Battleship, a game in which I could never be defeated.

One day Junior came over and said Crissy was up in the apartment puking, and I said, "That's no good." I followed him up there, and I thought as I walked into their place, I've got to be committing some kind of crime right now. Crissy was in their small bathroom with the door locked, and I said, "What's happening in there, dude?" and she said, "Leave me alone," and I said, "As long as you aren't dying," and she said, "I'm not dying. I got my period," and Junior and I looked at each other, surprised and kind of giggling, and she shouted, "Are you laughing at me?" and I said, "No way, man," and held my hand over my mouth, and I said, "Well, what do you want me to do?" and she said, "Nothing," and I could tell she was crying, and I said, "For real, Crissy, I have sisters. It's no big deal. Do you want me to do something?" and she said, "I need some of those pads, I guess," and I said, "Not a problem, man," and looked down at Junior and said, "Be cool. I'll be back in a minute," and I went down to the corner store and bought a box of superabsorbent pads from the Mexican grocery. I brought them upstairs, went into Junior and Crissy's, knocked on the bathroom door, and said, "Mission successful," and in a minute she opened up the door and then closed it fast. Junior and I rolled our eyes and sat on the sofa, and he said, "Do you want to see my room?" and I said, "Sure," and I followed him. It was all blue and white like any little boy's room except that there were these beautiful glass displays of all these real butterflies. They had been mounted and were hanging on the walls. I said, "You like butterflies, huh?" and he said, "They are my inheritance," very formal like that, and I said, "Really," and he said, "Yeah."

"What do you mean, your inheritance?"

"They were a wedding present to my mom before she died."

"Whatever happened to your dad?" I asked.

"Nobody knows. These butterflies are all mine, though."

"Well, they're top notch," I said.

"Yeah," he agreed.

"Did you know that there are scales on their wings?" he asked.

"How's that?" I said.

"Tiny scales, like fish," he said and pointed at one of the glass boxes. "Here, take a look." He handed me a small plastic magnifying glass, the kind you get in a cereal box, and I held it up to my eye and stared down at a huge orange and black butterfly the size of a crow. There, along its wings, were hundreds and thousands of tiny scales, just like the kid had said.

"Yep. See that, the blue one, below the wing? When you look at it like that, there is a secret."

"A secret?" I looked at the big blue and orange one, squinting to see.

"Yeah. If you look close, there's one that's a little heart," he said.

I squinted my eyes, and with the reflection from the daylight, it did look like one of the scales was a small orange heart, a tiny one. I wondered how long this kid had stared at the poor thing to see something like that.

"Wow, that's pretty neat," I said. "You're a smart kid, Junior."

"I eat brain foods," he said back.

"They work," I said.

"My dad," he said with a nod, "he stole these for my mom. He was a security guard at the Field Museum."

"That's true love," I said.

"I know," he said back.

6

At the beginning of that spring, Hannah had begun to come over when she was not drunk, and we would have very good conversations, such as how she had recently been accused of fraud at Ahoy There, Mateys! for signing herself a big tip on a credit card bill when one of her customers didn't leave her anything. Sometimes she would make coffee at my house, with my machine, and it seemed like we were a real couple. In the middle of us talking, she'd give me that look, with the big hungry eyes and the red freckles throbbing with lust, and I'd stand up to attack her, and she'd just get up and run out of the place. It was crazy. She would come over and start saying really racy stuff, dirty dreams she had had, porno movies she had seen, and she'd start kissing me, and when I would respond, she'd zip up her pants and run out, laughing. I thought maybe she had gone mental or maybe I could handle her only after she had been drinking, but it began to get more and more frustrating.

"I want to do it at my place," she said finally.

"That is out of the question," I said.

"Come on. It will be fun. It'll be exciting."

"Not if Bob walks in. It will be over then."

"So what if it's over? What do you care?"

"I dunno," I said. "I care."

"Bah," she said. "You are just like him." I went to grab her, but she ran out into the hall. She had a flowery dress on, and she lifted it up and flashed me the small white sheen of her panties. I stopped and watched her run down the stairs laughing.

7

One night after she came home from work, we were playing the board game Hijacked! and in the middle of a negotiation round, Hannah leaped up, threw her shoes at me, and ran out of the apartment. I stood, staring at the emptiness of the door frame, and then walked out into the hall. On the stairwell were her nylons. On the next flight, her white blouse and eye patch. On the landing, her white brassiere. On the basement steps, her black skirt and red neckerchief. And opening the door to the laundry, the overhead lights flickering and fading, I saw she was sitting on top of the washer, smiling, in her white panties, almost completely naked.

"You're going to get us in trouble," I said.

"I don't care," she said, wrapping her arms around my neck.

We were kissing and then she whispered, "I want romance," all breathy in my ear. "I want to be courted," she hummed. "I want you to be the man of my dreams."

"I just want you to be the girl that never gets sick of me," I said, and she smirked, biting my neck quickly.

8

A few days later, Bob, the husband, was dressed in a hockey jersey and was kind of drunk. He grabbed me by the neck as I went down to the laundry room and said, "We're gonna slaughter Montreal," and I saw the shiny patch of baldness Hannah had complained about, the black hair rising from beneath his white T-shirt along the back, and all I could think to say was "You bet, Bob."

Later, I was sitting upstairs in my apartment in the crummy green chair, feeling sick from the guilt for some reason and wondering who I thought I was exactly, doing what I had been doing, kidding myself that somehow I was the better man in anything. It suddenly occurred to me, this very bad thought, that anybody could love somebody for a few minutes, an hour, but what happened when it came to measuring love in terms of days, weeks, months? How could you be so sure then? What the hell could you even do to show somebody you cared after ten years of marriage? It seemed pretty hopeless to even bother about, but that's what I was thinking. I was very much in love with this woman and desperate to do something.

As proof of the possibility of our love, I decided I would surprise Hannah at work with some flowers, because that's real romance, right? I went to Ahoy There, Mateys! which was two buses away. By the time I got there, the flowers were looking like ruffled old blue and pink ladies, and when I walked in, Hannah, all dolled up in her pirate outfit, looked up, crossed her eyes, and frowned as the delicious aroma of fried seafood mugged me. She came up to the greasy yellow plastic booth I was sitting in and sat across from me; she held her face in her hands and sighed. I handed her the flowers, and she smiled and inhaled deeply.

"Well, may I take your order, sir?" she said with a big smile.

"I just want you," I said.

"That's sweet," she said, blinking her big fake eyelashes at me.

"No, I mean it," I said. "I want to try, just you and me."

Hannah laughed and patted my hand. "I told you already. I'm married." She grinned and then winked. "You can still have me, though." She touched my hand again. "What else could you need?"

I felt my heart go. Here I was trying so hard, so hard, and she just wouldn't see it. "Just forget it," I said, unfolding my wallet. "Just give me a shrimp basket. And a cola."

"That's it?" she asked, crinkling up her eyebrows. "That's it? You're not gonna even fight for me? I thought you were going to be the man of my dreams."

"Hannah," I said, "I'll be whatever you want me to be. You want me to fight for you, I'll do it. I thought that's what I'd been doing. I mean, that's why I came here today—to show you, you know, what you mean to me."

"You just ordered something to eat! You're doing a lousy job of convincing me."

"Well," I said, "you're not doing such a swell job yourself, lady."

Hannah shot me a dirty look, I mean a real dirty look, where her eyes almost crossed, and then she got up, went behind the counter, threw my flowers in the trash, piled my greasy orange shrimp in one of those red plastic baskets, and flung it down on the table in front of me angrily.

"Thank you. Come again," she said and turned her back on me.

10

While Junior and Crissy were doing their homework a few days later, all of us sitting on my floor watching *Jeopardy!* to which Crissy knew most of the answers, there was a knock, a light one. I knew it was Hannah, so I asked the kids, "How do I look?"

"Like a bum," Crissy said.

I said, "Crissy, you're going to be working a very unfulfilling job and be very, very lonely if you keep being so mean."

I stood up and opened the door. Hannah was there and already she was a little tipsy, because she reached in and started kissing me hard—she tasted like margaritas—and then she looked up and saw the kids. Junior and Crissy didn't know what to make of her, because she really did look a little weird, all dressed up as a pirate with her eye patch on and her makeup runny and her, well, a little loopy.

She said, "Who are these kids?" and I said, "They live upstairs. We hang out, you know. We do homework and stuff."

Hannah flipped up her eye patch and trained one red eye on me, as if suddenly she had no idea who I was. "You," she said, pointing her finger at me. "You are very funny." I took her hand and led her into the kitchen to sit down. "I came here to tell you I've been waiting down in the laundry room the last few nights, and you haven't been there," she said.

"I know," I said. "I don't feel right about Bob."

"What's changed? What's different?" she asked. "It was all good a few days ago, right?"

"I dunno. I can't change your mind," I said. "I've tried, but I can't." Then it hit me. I grabbed Hannah's freckled white hand, jerked her out of her seat, ran into the front room, and asked Junior, "Is your place unlocked?" He nodded, and I pulled Hannah up the stairs and into Junior and Crissy's place. We walked right into Junior's blue and white bedroom, and I pointed out the butterflies to her.

"What's all this? A butterfly collection?" she asked. She tapped on one of the glass frames and stared at it.

"Here, look, look at this," I said, pointing to the big blue and orange one. "See, it's got a heart on its wing." I handed her the magnifying glass. Hannah looked at it and nodded, not seeing it, because she turned and squinted, frowning.

"I want to ask you something," she said. "How can you be sure I won't ever cheat on you?"

"I don't know," I said. "I'm just sure."

"Well, I'm not so sure," she said. "I might be ruined for life now. A good-looking guy left me his number at work the other day, and I thought about calling him."

"Well, that's okay," I said, "because you didn't call. Because I'm sure enough for the both of us."

"But how can you ever be sure if I'm not?" she said.

And I was going to say, *See this butterfly? Look. See the little heart? It's one in a million, but it's there. It means you and me, we might be all right. See?* But she didn't, so I didn't. I just held her hand a very long time and made believe that the best thing I had in my crummy life wasn't just about ending.

"I've got to go home and sleep it off," she said, kissing my cheek. I nodded and walked her out and went back down to my place. Crissy and Junior stared up at me, seeing by my droopy eyes that I was somehow defeated. I sat on the sofa a long time without saying anything, watching *Jeopardy!* and feeling dumber than usual for not knowing any of the answers to anything. Junior was still on the floor. He looked over his shoulder, saw I was feeling blue, and scribbled something in his lap. Then, very slyly, very slowly, he folded up the small white piece of paper, turned, and handed me a secret.

1

It is bad to go to the airport to steal strangers' bags. I know this. My brother, Junior, on the other hand, he goes up there every day and comes home with someone else's suitcase. It's unbelievable to me. He's just a kid, you know, a sophomore in high school, and like everybody, I guess, he may be looking to find something he has lost. I don't know. When I find him sitting on the couch, playing those lame video games, wearing what must be some strange old white dude's black and white wing tips or strutting around the place in some purple Hawaiian cabana shirt, it makes me nervous. When I see the kid eating cereal out of the box, wearing a priest's cowl and collar, a getup that must have definitely been stolen from some poor third world missionary, I get a little worried. Why? Because he's been doing it for a while. He goes up to the airport every day, or almost every day, right after his last class. He rides his bicycle the nine or ten blocks, locks his bike up, and finds a terminal that's busy—you know, real crowded. Then he just sits there and waits for the planes to come in. He looks out the terminal window and watches the planes taking off and landing, listening to the sounds, checking out all the people. When the planes come in, he goes to the baggage claim, right, and he stands there and watches. He stands there and watches and stands there and watches, and he waits and waits, and then he goes and steals people's suitcases. He takes their luggage. I don't know why he does it. I just don't know what is wrong with him.

2

"What is wrong with you?" I ask across the dinner table. The dinner table is not a real dinner table, it is more of a long end table. It was in the trash behind our building, and we needed something to eat on because the carpet in the apartment was coated with crumbs and food and looked worn and ratty. It is our apartment, his and mine, which is why everything looks so lousy.

"I don't know what's wrong with me," he says, lowering his head, hiding behind his brown hair. His hair is bad-looking. It is like a bowl cut that my mother used to make him get. He doesn't use any products in it. He doesn't care how he looks, like for girls or anything. He is wearing a red cardigan sweater. He is sixteen. He shouldn't have a bowl cut and a cardigan sweater, man. He should have rock T-shirts. He should have shirts that are offensive, even to me. He should have drastic hair that looks stupid. He should have loud, snotty friends that call up and try to get him to do dumb things, like getting drunk and sneaking into bars. That, too, has me worried—his lack of weirdness and his lack of friends, you know.

"I'm sorry," he says. "I'll stop doing it." He puts his fork down and looks like he might begin crying. The macaroni I have cooked may be just that bad.

"Okay, do that," I say and nod and try to ignore it. Maybe he really has gone crazy. Maybe you really do need two parents and all that. I don't know. I know I have had to deal with the exact same things: father taking off, mother putting all our clothes out on the lawn and telling us we needed to find a new place to live. But I am okay with it. I can hold down a job and don't need to resort to stealing people's special, sacred traveling things.

"You are messing up people's vacations, man," I tell him.

"You don't know that," he says.

"I do know that. I know if I worked all year and only got two weeks off and I went to Chicago and someone stole my bag from the airport, I would be pretty angry, man. I would shout at my wife and kids, and it would ruin the only time I'm getting off the whole year, man."

"Listen," he says. "I'm not bothering anyone. It's just clothes and stuff like that mostly."

"But what are you doing with them, man?" I ask. "I mean, how many suitcases do you already have?"

"Eighteen."

"Eighteen? What is with you? Are you really crazy?"

"I don't know. Ask Moms," he says.

"Low blow, my man," I say, and he gets up from the table. Junior is the reason we are living in a one-bedroom apartment now. Maybe it is okay for me, because I am nineteen, almost twenty, but it is not okay for him. One day a few months back, when we were still living with our mom, Junior was arguing with her about getting a later curfew—for what, I don't know—but she wouldn't budge. So he picked up the phone, pretended to dial, and said, "Hello, Dad? Yeah. Mom won't let me stay out until twelve." Then he pretended to continue the conversation. "Is it okay with you that I stay out? It is? Awesome. Thanks, Dad." Then he hung up, and my mom tossed a plate, a plate with meat loaf on it—good meat loaf, my mom's meat loaf, which has an egg in the center of it, which is really very excellent even though it sounds weird. She tossed the plate at his head, but instead it ended up breaking the head off the statue of the good luck Virgin Mary sitting next to the sink. The thing is, our dad has been gone for a while, and the stunt, the imaginary phone call, and then the beheading of the Virgin Mary was too much for my mom to take. But like an idiot I was laughing, and she pointed, turned, closed her eyes—the eyes that are always dark and circled in years of sadness—and said, "The two of you, I am done with! I am done with the two of you!"

The next day when I came home from work, Junior was sitting on the front lawn next to drawers and drawers full of his clothes and my clothes, and he was crying. We stayed at my pal Eddie's house for a while, but he had illicit things happening there, which I did not think was cool for a sixteen-year-old to have to deal with, things like his ex-wife, this woman with blue mascara who hung out with all these drug dealers from Blue Island and who came barging into the house in the middle of the night shouting, "Eddie, if you're with that girl from Twenty-sixth Street, you're dead." Nobody should be sleeping on a couch dealing with that kind of stuff when you're sixteen, you know? So we waited until we had enough for a security deposit and moved into the Colonial Apartments, which is exactly three blocks from the spot where *it* happened, where my dad left us. So I have to drive three blocks in the opposite direction to go around it, but I love my brother, and that is the price I am willing to pay for our sanity—that, and I have met a nice white girl named Carrie who works at the Laundromat where we drop our clothes off to be cleaned. She is tall and very pale. She has orange freckles everywhere. She is going to community college at Daley. She likes to read the books she's been assigned in class out loud to me—you know, late at night when we are lying on the couch and my brother is snoring or fake-snoring in our one and only bedroom and the TV is on, but only for light, and I put my head on her hip. She reads some psychology book out loud, but she does it with an English accent, but not on purpose. It's just something she does. She is reading, and I close my eyes and wonder what the heck to do about my little brother, and I think he is in our room thinking what else he is going to steal.

3

At the stoplight across from the Ford City shopping center, at the beginning of the summer when I was eight, my dad turned to my mom, blinked, and said, "I'm sorry. I can't do this anymore." He then jumped out of the driver's seat and disappeared into the haze of late silvery traffic and the muggy summer heat. Like I said, I was eight at the time. Junior was five. We were both singing along to the Beach Boys, my brother's voice high pitched and warbly like a broken whistle, the sound reverberating like a bee buzzing in his missing teeth. He had had his nose broken, four teeth knocked out, and his arm fractured that summer.

I had pushed him out of our front tree.

My mother shouted something, some Spanish cussword that probably wasn't even that bad, considering, you know, something that wouldn't make you blush even if you heard your friend's mom say it. I turned and looked out the back window of the station wagon, which we referred to as *el coche fúnebre,* the hearse, because my brother's guinea pigs were run down by it when my father had come roaring up the driveway the day he got his last raise. In the window, I caught the last glimpse ever of my dad—gold sunglasses, brand-new black beard on his dark face, brown permanent curly hair, red windbreaker, dirty work pants coated in grease—as he was thumbing a ride in the opposite direction. He saw me, nodded, looked down, and then hopped into a metallic blue T-top Camaro that was being driven by some blond somebody with long hair—a man or a girl, I don't know—but just as "Barbara Ann" ended, my dad disappeared. It became the central event in all our lives, my brother's and my mom's and mine, then and now. It was the moment when I found out that anything could happen, that no one was predictable. The moment when everything got very bad and then very strange for me.

4

I work the line at the Solo Plastics factory like my old man used to. Like I said, I am nineteen now. It's okay work, really. My dad was a repair engineer; he was the guy you called when the assembly line got busted. Things are always getting busted at the old plastics factory. Why? Because no one else likes working there. *Es horrible,* it is murder. I've seen people cut their hands open with box knives on purpose, just to get out of an hour of work. I've stumbled into the bathroom and seen guys doing huge lines of cocaine, right off the bathroom sinks. Why? It's not the job itself that's so bad.

They're smart at Solo. They keep you moving. There are four positions in the assembly line: the guy who pulls the molded cups from the molding machine and sets them on the conveyor belt, separating out the burned or malformed ones; the guy who sends the cups through the rimmer, which, as you can guess, adds a rim; the guy who counts them into sections of ten; and then the guy who bags them and stuffs them in a box. They make you switch every two hours so you don't go crazy, which is nice. The only problem is the sound. The press and molding machines are so loud, you can scream at the top of your lungs, close your eyes and holler, and a dude two feet away can't hear you. So no chitchat. No talking to anybody. The noise drives some people crazy. I love it. It's like when we were kids and lived even closer to the airport, only like four blocks away, and when other kids came over and the whole front room would shake from the planes, my brother and I wouldn't even notice. This one kid, Miguel Gasta, who went to our school but lived in Burbank, he started crying one time because a picture fell off the wall. Junior and me, we didn't even notice what was happening. We just kept on playing.

I get on that assembly line and I sing as loud as I can, songs like "Quizás, Quizás, Quizás" or "Roxanne" by the Police, that part where the singer hollers,

"Raaaaaaaaaaaaox-anne." You can holler that all day, and no one can say you're not singing good. Also, well, it gives me time to think, which is okay sometimes, but sometimes it's not so great.

Let's say you are on the line that makes red plastic cups, the kind you drink from at your friend's high school party, if you're lucky, or the kind maybe you have at your little cousin's baptism. You know the party I am talking about: the one when you are a lonely teenager, the one when your *tío* sneaks you beers and your older girl cousin takes you for a ride to go pick up more ice and she has her own Mustang convertible and lets you smoke some of her cigarette and there is that little red lipstick mark from her lips on the cigarette and that's funny, you know, and you don't care that she is listening to her lame house music because this is the best you've felt in a long time, which seems like your whole life. It's just you and your girl cousin who has a Mustang and who is older and pretty and has been given whatever she's asked for and you. Your father is still missing, and you wonder about it even when you know it's dumb and useless to keep on wondering, and she has the top down and her black hair is blowing and she asks if you have any real girlfriends yet and you say, "Sure, man," though you do not, except the white girl freshman year, Amy, the one you terrorized by asking out every day for three months straight until you made her cry, and then her mom called you and asked you to please stop asking. But all that is over, it is in the rearview mirror, it is in the past. That good girl cousin switches the radio station, and it is your favorite song, which at that moment is "Sister Christian," though you haven't got a clue who sings it. Your head is cold from her having the top down, but it doesn't matter, and you think maybe that white girl, Amy, will see you riding with this older girl cousin in a convertible and think twice about saying no next time. Just then you fly past the corner where it happened, you know, where your dad just hopped out like he was going to spank you for talking smart back to him, but instead he walked across the street and lifted up his thumb, and when your cousin asks, "What's the matter, *niño?*" and you say your head is cold and "Can we put the top up maybe?"

When I think too much and when things start on fire, which happens a lot at Solo because of all the heat and plastic, are the things that bother me the most about working. That and I'm nineteen, almost twenty, and a lot of other nineteen-year-olds are going to college and getting with girls, and I am working a full-time job and have an idiot brother and an apartment to take care of already.

5

When we were in grammar school, there was a pumpkin-carving contest every Halloween. Every year, without fail, Junior and I won either first or second or third place. The trick was that my mother carved the pumpkins for us. We were not allowed to do much more than empty the big orange rinds of their floppy yellow guts. No one caught on that my mom was cheating, like the teachers or principal or anything. There is a photo somewhere in my mom's house of Junior and me, and we have won the pumpkin contest again, and we both have ribbons and are smiling. He's on one end of this table where all the winners are standing and smiling, and me, I'm on the other end. Our pumpkins are both painted and look exactly the same, you know, except his is an Indian and mine is Dracula, but the features and colors, they're all the same. I look at that picture and wonder how none of the teachers or the principal ever caught on, and then I think maybe they knew all along and were just humoring us, right? Like they knew that my mom was the one carving the pumpkins every year but thought that that was really sad, you know, like desperate, maybe because they had heard about my dad leaving, because everyone knew about it, so they just let it go, you know, they just let us keep on winning out of pity.

I think about that photo all the time, and it makes me angry, being pitied. It makes me angrier than my dad actually leaving.

When I came home from work one day, Junior was on the couch, and he was wearing a beekeeper's outfit, the whole getup: boots, gloves, suit, mask. He was sitting in the beekeeper's outfit watching TV.

"What's with the getup?" I asked, standing before him with my arms across my chest.

"I found it in a suitcase," he said and went back to watching TV. I think maybe he was either feeling bad or trying very hard to get me to think about how bad he was feeling. Either way, I got mad. I got mad and didn't know what to do, so I didn't say anything.

6

I have not talked to my mother in months. The last time I called her, she hung up on me. I said my brother was being a pain. He was staying out late, stealing stuff, not doing his homework. I said I was about to murder him. She said, "I don't know what it is you think you are doing or who you are supposed to be.

You didn't raise him. I did. The two of you, you two are nothing but ungrace-ful." Then the line went click, and I thought, Did she just say "ungraceful" or "ungrateful"? But I did not call her back to ask.

7

I got a phone call from Midway saying Junior had been picked up for trying to make off with someone's suitcase. Big news. I went down there, pulled the anx-ious, squinty-eyed security guard to the side, and said, "I'm going to level with you. Both our parents died in a plane crash last year. It's a mental thing for him." The heavy guard nodded and then apologized for the whole incident.

8

One year for Christmas when I was a teenager, we got mysterious Christmas presents in the mail. We assumed they were from him, meaning my pops. I was like sixteen at the time. My brother was in junior high. My dad sent me a plastic watch, the kind you win at carnivals, and it had Spider-Man on it. My brother got a furry white teddy bear. I kept that watch in a junk box in my room, with all the plastic wallets and shark teeth and saint medals and blue ribbons I had ever received, until I got afraid that the girl I was dating, Angie, my first real girlfriend, would somehow, without reason, come over to my house when I wasn't home, look through my room, find the watch, and break up with me. I have been afraid of that, too, for a long time—of being found out, of being exposed for being something I'm not. I thought about it a long time after the phone call with my mom and later, after Junior got busted. Maybe she was right.

Maybe I was trying to be something I was not, and here, here was the proof. It seemed no matter what happened, no matter what I said, the kid could just not stop himself from stealing other people's things, and in the end, I really wasn't doing anything to try to stop it from happening.

9

Two days after Junior got busted, I got called into the health office at the factory in the middle of my shift. Immediately, I thought for sure that Junior had gone crazy and been shot by the police robbing a bank. Instead, a big doe-eyed nurse handed me a form to fill out and said, "We need a urine sample. You are being tested for drug use."

"Well, I can tell you right now, I don't do that stuff."

She clicked her teeth, looked me up and down like a judge, and said, "We still need a sample."

"No problem," I said. She handed me the plastic cup, and I went into the little bathroom to try to, you know, go, but I couldn't. I sat in there for like ten minutes, until the nurse knocked and asked, "Are you all right?" and I said, "I don't know. I don't have to go," and she said, "Well, I need a sample," and I said, "Well, nothing's happening," and she said, "Well, that's going to be a problem," and I said, "Maybe if you stopped talking," and she said, "I can wait all day," and I asked, "Can I just go back to work?" and she said, "Not without a sample," and I thought, This is how they are going to get me. I will get fired for not being able to go to the bathroom on command, and my brother and me will get tossed out into the streets. I will have to work at McDonald's, and he will become a crack smoker. I have dealt with everything else pretty okay, and they are going to get me to give up because of this? But already I had begun to go to the bathroom, and I could hear the nurse outside clapping.

The drug test came back negative, which it should have because I do not do drugs, but for some reason I was sure I was going to be accused of something. So I decided we all needed to celebrate. Junior, Carrie, and I went to the Olive Garden on Pulaski. We lounged in the fake Italian setting. We loaded up on bread sticks and free salad. We ate until we couldn't speak. I thought, Olive Garden! You have saved us with your imitation Italian cooking! As the dessert tray was being shown around, Junior looked up at Carrie and me, his eyes twinkling mischievously, and said, "Do you want to know a secret?"

Carrie nodded and said, "Okay."

"Luis used to have a Spider-Man watch."

"I did not. Our dad gave it to me. I never even wore it."

"But you kept it."

"Big deal," I said.

"And he stares at himself naked in the mirror."

"Great. This is the kind of conversation you want to have?" I asked.

Junior shrugged and blinked his eyes. He looked at me, then at Carrie, who was busy with a big chocolate tiramisu. "You guys having sex yet?"

"Junior!" I shouted. "Grow up, man."

"I can hear you out there," he whispered. "Talking. Saying things. Talking about me."

Carrie's pale freckles immediately went bright pink.

"You are acting like a child, man," I said. "How would you like it if I embarrassed you?"

"I wouldn't mind. I don't have anything to hide."

I turn to Carrie and blurt out, "Junior likes to steal suitcases from the airport."

"Big deal." Junior laughed.

"Why do you do that, Junior?" Carrie asked.

"I don't know. Something to do." He was acting very suave, very cool.

"I think it's because you want to punish those people for leaving," Carrie said, frowning.

I thought about it for a minute, and it made sense. "You're a little weirdo," I said.

"No, that's not why."

"Then why?" Carrie asked.

"I don't know why," he said. "I like looking at families and stuff."

"Families and stuff?" I asked.

"When you take it home, the suitcase, it's like family stuff inside. You figure out what kind of family it is, if it is good or bad or happy or whatever."

Carrie leaned in, interested. "Are most of them happy?" she asked.

Junior shook his head. "I don't think so."

"Why not?" I asked.

"Almost every suitcase has pills, you know, like sleeping pills and stuff. And the pictures. From vacations. Nobody seems like they want to be there."

"See," I said. "You don't have it so bad." From the look on Carrie's face, I immediately wished that I hadn't said it.

10

About two weeks after that, Carrie and I were on the sofa. It was late. I could hear Junior snoring in the other room. It was his actual snoring, not his fake kind, which you can tell because they are long snores and deep and twitchy. His snoring has become worse since the time we were kids and I shoved him out of the tree. At that moment, though, Carrie and I were kissing. She was reading something out loud—I don't know what, some psychology book—and every so often she took her gum out of her mouth, stuck it on the plastic sofa cover, and we would kiss.

"This is nice," she said.

"You bet," I said.

"You're nice," she said.

"You're nicer," I repeated.

"Okay, you win," she said.

"What do I win?" I asked.

"Me," she said, and we kissed again. "Luis, how come you won't ever come by my place?"

I looked up and pointed toward the bedroom where Junior was snoring.

"He's sixteen. He can take care of himself," she said.

"Unfortunately, he can't. He blew up the microwave yesterday. He tried microwaving a ham sandwich in tinfoil."

"That's not so bad," she said and smiled.

"He's lonely, you know. He doesn't have any friends," I said.

"I want you to come over before I have to leave," she said. She took her gum off the plastic sofa cover and popped it back in her mouth.

"Leave? When are you leaving?" I muttered.

"Two weeks."

"Two weeks!" I stood up and paced. "Where are you going, if I may ask?"

"I got into the nurse's program in Arizona. I leave in two weeks."

"Arizona? You weren't even going to tell me about this?" I asked.

"That's what this is," she said.

"Well, this is not good," I said. "This is not good at all." Then: "Arizona?"

"What do you want me to do about it?" she asked. "I'm not too happy about it."

"But you're the one deciding to go to Arizona," I said.

"Of course I am, Luis. This is what I've been going to school for, right? I'd be a total idiot if I didn't go."

"Well, what am I supposed to say to that?"

"How about congratulations?"

"Well, congratulations. Send me some rocks or something."

I sat back down and wouldn't look at her. She sighed. I turned my head in the opposite direction. She sighed again. In a minute, like magic, we got back to kissing.

11

I decided to throw Carrie a going-away party. She was without a doubt the best girl I ever dated, so I got some streamers and some balloons and told Junior that we were having a going-away party and that I was cooking dinner, which was something I never did. Our diet was mainly burned macaroni and pizza from the place down the street. I decided to do something easy and bake some chicken. I got the recipe from a magazine that was left in the apartment entryway. I went out and got the ingredients. Things were marinating. I put things in the oven, and they were cooking. I looked up, and it was seven o'clock already. The doorbell rang. Carrie was there, smiling. She was looking beautiful in a pink sweater. I took her hand and led her inside. She flicked a red balloon with her finger. She was sad. I was sad, but I didn't want to give in to it. I took the chicken out of the oven. I called into the bedroom for Junior. There was no answer. I opened the bedroom door. It was empty.

"I told him seven," I kept repeating.

Carrie and I waited. We looked down at our hands, awkward, soon to be strangers again. I wanted to kill my little brother for making me sit there waiting with her like that. I stood up. I made a decision. "I'll be right back," I said.

"Where are you going?" she asked.

"I am going to bring him back," I said and tore at the closet for my jacket.

12

At the end of the B terminal, there was my little brother, *el insecto,* wearing his blue stocking cap and staring at a family of people talking in German, hugging each other wildly.

"Junior, what the heck are you doing here?" I shouted, shaking him.

"I don't know. Just being by myself."

"We had plans, pal. We had plans. Going-away party? Dinner at seven? Seven? Remember?"

"I thought you'd rather be alone, you know, with her."

"If I wanted to be alone, I wouldn't have invited you," I shouted again.

"Well, I don't know. Maybe you did it just to be nice."

"To be nice? You're my brother. I'm not supposed to do things to be nice to you. I do them because I have to."

"See. That's it. You asked me out of pity, man."

"Of course I asked you out of pity. You don't do anything, so I thought, What the heck. Carrie's leaving tomorrow, you know. I thought you would like to say good-bye."

"Why would I care? She's only nice to me because she likes you."

"That's not true," I said, patting his back.

"Don't pat my back," he said, crossing his arms in front of his chest. "I'm not a kid."

"See, you are a kid. To me, anyway. You know, you're like my weird little brother, and I don't mind. I'm happy you're my brother, but you can't go on being like this. You've got to snap out of it."

"Snap out of what?" he asked.

"Snap out of being weird and lonely all the time."

"I am not weird and lonely."

"Junior, you're a weird little lonely guy."

"I don't try to be weird."

"Well, I don't know, but you do weird things. Like why do you come here all the time, man?" I shouted at him. "It's depressing. It's a little mental, you know?"

"Because," he murmured, "I like seeing the people."

"Seeing the people?"

"I like seeing the people. When they come home to their friends and kids and stuff. I like seeing them walk out after they land. When they hug and everything. I like seeing that."

"You like watching them come home?"

"Yeah, I guess," he said.

"Wow," I said. "Listen, Junior, listen, you're going to be fine. We're all going to be fine here." I hugged him and felt his puffy winter jacket as it smashed against my face. Outside, planes were taking off and landing. I got this strange idea in my head just then when I was hugging him and watching the planes take off and land. I got this idea that for some reason I should be thankful for my father leaving. If my dad never left, my mom would never have gone crazy, and, well, my brother and I would not be living together and I would never have met Carrie, and this moment with my brother and me standing here like this would definitely never have happened. I was suddenly thankful for all of it, the comings and goings. I thought I would tell my brother about it sometime later when he wanted to talk about it, maybe, and I started to hope that this moment, this one here, would be the one we looked back on. It was too soon to tell, I guess, and we settled for standing there for a moment, watching the whole world take off and land.

MR. SONG

I lived next door to Mr. Song. Yes, the one from the radio show. At the time of our acquaintance, we struck a kind of arrangement whereby I would leave small paper bags containing decorative bottles of various grain alcohol and fruit liqueur in front of his door early in the evening, say around eight o'clock, right before a bachelor goes out to, say, pick up his date. Then after a cheap movie at the Esquire or some dinner downtown maybe, I would come home and knock on my neighbor's door twice, then bring my date into my own crumb-bum living place and allow ourselves to wait. Slowly, I would be engaged in dimming the lights, arranging the pillows on the sofa, drawing the best devilish smile I could without trying to give a hint, and then, surely and soon enough, there would appear, just like that, enchantment.

Margaret was a girl I hardly knew, a big beautiful redhead who I had met at a small cocktail party hosted by some bum at work—work being the no-account consulting game whereby ingenious stiffs like me toil to save plutocratic institutions from shelling out any more cents for their workers' pensions than they have to. At my job I was an absolute no one, a complete zero. I could walk down the maze of rows of tiny white cubicles, so much like bordered compartments of some senile, money-hungry heart, and no one would recognize me. If I ran into my boss or my department supervisor on my long tours around the office, there would always be a moment of awkward silence where they would try to remember my name, and when they never could, they would say, "Good job on that Abramson report," and I would nod, because in that business, the business of nickels and dimes, the business of the future interest of a penny, beauty lay in the soft configuration of numbers and not in the telling features of some stranger's face.

I, on the other hand, have always been more interested in the aesthetic of certain unknown beautiful faces. Margaret was a looker with red hair that spilled down her back like the most glorious tropical volcano explosion you could ever hope to discover during a vacation. I was watching her the whole night: the way she was holding her drink, a vodka and cranberry, and spilling it slightly while she was smiling and laughing, which was a good sign, because that meant she was actually smiling and laughing and not one of those kinds of gals who will talk your head off and smile and laugh when they don't mean it because you certainly haven't said anything funny, and there's nothing worse in the world to me than a gal who's a phony. Around midnight, when the party began to break up and Margaret the redhead was climbing into her soft, fur-collared jacket, I pulled an old one that every lousy Ivy Leaguer knows but thinks is too shameful to use. But I figure if a trick is old, it has to be good. I approached and crossed behind as she was pulling her arm into her soft white sleeve and, zip-zap, she ended up spilling my wine all over me and staining my sweater and, oh, the spoilage, oh, the humanity. Margaret, the dear, was all red hair and full of the most beautiful silver apologies. "Will it stain, you think?" her voice like choir bells as she asked, and me, being chivalrous, replying, "It's no matter," and her saying, "Well, it's horrible of me. I'm a horrible person, really," and me saying something swell like, "No, it's horrible of me that I should have upset you like this," and her closing the deal with, "Well, here's my number and address. Please promise me you'll send a bill," and me, unable to take my eyes off the freckles on her neck the whole time, simply stopping myself from smiling.

(I donate a box of clothes to the Salvation Army on account of this stunt every year. Dry cleaners have WANTED posters of me in their back room, I swear.)

Margaret, being a girl I caught with such an old trick, was sure to be charmed without end on the first date. Candlelight dinner, walk in the park. I touched the darling, most innocent path of her white wrist and remarked what a beautiful watch she was wearing and left the petting at that. In her heart she must have been crying—no, singing—thinking what a gentleman, what a catch, I was, but really what a bum. What a lousy no-good bum I am. And I mean it, friend.

Margaret was more than happy to see me on a second date. The second date she wore something off the shoulders that was a kind of easily translated message to me. I was an old tube radio—no, a foreign correspondent—picking up her gentle transmission, and the message was saying, "Tonight, more than anything in a thousand years of waiting, I want you to kiss me." So I did. In front of a fountain with a silver statue of Neptune in the center of it. I took out a quarter, said, "Did you know this fountain is magic?" tossed the quarter in, told her to close her eyes, and then I kissed her. Before she could argue, I said, "See, it works! I got much more than I could have ever wished for," which ended with more kissing and her sighing and then laying her head against my neck in the taxicab on the way back.

At this point I must argue on my behalf that clearly, clearly if a girl was so gullible as to fall for both of those ploys, she must have been a chiseler, a tramp, or a nun. A chiseler, well, whatever they get, they deserve, I say. If a girl is simply after your money clip, then whatever turmoil she creates, she's made herself. I've been with women like that, and the horrifying thing is the similarity they share with men who have one thing on their minds, an end—men like the kind I am, I guess. A tramp, well, a tramp is a sad kind of girl on her own, and it's usually best to steer as clear as possible only because, though she may not be lacking in fun, she always ends up in some kind of car wreck. A nun, well, a nun—Margaret might very well have been a nun, the kind of girl who is raised by nannies and spends summers with rich relatives in guarded estates in the country. Necking to her might have been the real thing, truly. Going on looks, she was a knockout, but it seemed that inside her beautiful head there could not have been anything but very lovely green vapors, and I guess I didn't know what else I should have expected.

I made a mistake is what I am saying at this point, I guess.

On the next date, our third date, I left a pint bottle of scotch in front of Mr. Song's door just before I went out and on the way back in with Margaret gave the indicative two knocks, took her fur-lined coat, and coaxed her to the sofa; the clip of flame-red hair came undone, and my heart swaggered. In moments like that I doubt everything I'm doing, the games, the tricks, and so forth. A moment like that, with the hair tumbling down the shoulders, will make you forget everything. But then you remember the hair clip being removed and your date slowly removing her shoes. It is just some other kind of trick and has very little to do with comfort and a lot more to do with, simply and effectively, enchanting you.

At that moment, more than anything in the world, I began to pray that Mr. Song would begin his singing, because I was swimming. To be honest, with her shoes off and her bare feet inches away and her red hair lighting a fire along the sofa and her asking, "Are you all right, darling? You look flush," well, I was swimming. I asked if she wanted a drink, she nodded, and I stalled some more, mixing the highballs. Just when I felt about ready to settle down permanently and kneel at this beauty's feet, silence hung in the spaces behind the thin plaster walls with such heavy weight that I felt matrimony nearly setting in. There was still no singing.

Usually Mr. Song starts out with something tender like "That Old Feeling," something nostalgic, not too serious, capricious, yes, but full of the definite implications and intentions of love. Whereupon I would, feigning surprise, declare, "There's my rowdy neighbor, Mr. Song, howling at the stars again," and stretch one long arm around the victim's neck, then ask, "Did you know he had his own radio program in the forties?" Then there might be a nice interlude, a procession into "It's Always You" or some delicate Gershwin, "Long

Ago and Far Away," where my fingers would begin to toy with the string of pearls around the young lady's neck. Mr. Song's voice would rise, growing more powerful and much more brassy, like a trumpet shaking loose some of its dust and rust, and by the time "Time after Time" was slowly sweeping through the tin vents and cheap plaster from the apartment beside mine, clasps would be unclasped, boundaries would be surpassed, and a soft cooing would be heard as a kind of accompaniment to each of Mr. Song's carefully chosen lines.

And still it went very wrong the other night.

Margaret, no dumb nun as I had guessed, caught me giving the two knocks on Mr. Song's door. I covered as best as I could, saying, "It's a sign we have. He gets worried about me. He's like a grandfather, I guess. I wouldn't want to keep him up all night waiting for me."

"Could I meet him?" she asked.

"Oh, he's probably indecent at the moment," I said, and she just shrugged and gave the old man's door another few knocks, until the rummy came to the door in his bathrobe, shaking his scotchy head, as confused as me, I guess.

"Hello." My date smiled. "I'm Margaret." Just like that, shaking his hand.

Mr. Song looked at the girl and then at me. His face was white and soft, with the lines of a bumpy pillow along his forehead. He had yellow whiskers on one side of his face and a blue vein along his knob nose, which was purple as a beetle. He cracked open one red eye, which was like parting a mussel from its shell, and muttered, "I'm ready," and then, "Is it showtime yet?"

Very quickly, without thinking, I said, "Well, I didn't want you to wait up for me. I'm home all right. So you can . . . go to bed, old pal."

"Good," he said and closed the door quickly, and that was that.

When we entered my apartment, I began stalling, trying to think of something to say, waiting, waiting, hoping, praying that the old man would start singing anyway. But there was nothing. There wasn't going to be anything tonight.

Margaret began to kiss me very softly on the mouth. Margaret did not wait. She began to unzip her dress, and I worked to unclasp her brassiere, gently running my hands along the top of her freckled chest. I felt like an adventurer embarking on a beatific snowbound expedition but without the supplies or resources I needed to pass the test, and just then I thought, Here, here is a girl who does not need tricks. Here is a girl for me.

I went along with it all very quickly, beginning to unbutton my pants.

"Would you put a record on?" she asked. "Something soft."

"Okay," I said. I got off the sofa and put on a Cole Porter record, letting the music slowly build in its blueness. I dimmed the lights and took a seat back on the sofa, giving her a smile, still hoping the old man would give us one song for experience anyway, but it did not matter. All the quiet things of the world were beginning to blossom with love right before me.

"I am trying to be brave," Margaret said.

"You are doing very well," I said back, kissing her arm all the way up to her neck.

"I am being very brave," she said again, and I looked up and saw she was crying. Small, soft, teacup-shaped tears were gently riding down her cheek. I leaned back, not knowing what to think, because from the way she was going,

I was pretty sure of one thing: Margaret was no nun. She was something I had never had in the apartment before, I think.

"The other night . . . at the fountain," she said.

"Yes?"

"I wished for this."

"So did I," I said, and for the first time all night it was the truth, which was a real moment for me, bum that I am. The record began to skip, and I went to fix it. When I came back to the couch, Margaret was trembling. In the soft crook of her elbow, her pulse was beating like a hidden rabbit, and I realized very quickly that I did not have the sincerity to handle something like this. We began to kiss again, and she was lying there, nude on my sofa, and I was beginning to undress when I heard her say, "My brother died . . . in the service last year," and it was a real queer thing to say, especially at a time like that. "It makes me see things. Things that aren't always there."

And so I began to realize this girl *was* seeing things, things that were the lies of things I had planted and things that were no good. I just sat there, and she kept on kissing me, whispering, but I just let the music block out any words she was saying. I was as stiff as a corpse, and she was asking me what was the matter, and I just listened to Cole Porter blaring out of the hi-fi. Then Margaret was yelling and cursing at me, and I just stood there in the dim lights as she began to dress, and within a moment the soft fur-collared coat was back on and I was watching Margaret climb into a taxi and the red hair was disappearing behind the glass, down the street, around the corner, and out of time and out of reach, for me at least.

I walked back upstairs, knocked on Mr. Song's door, and found him amid empty bottles, lying on the floor beneath a flock of white moths. Without a word I lifted him gently under the neck, dragged him into bed, and shut off the light. I sat in my apartment and stared at the walls, listening to him breathe, thinking. Finally, I watched the city awake from the tranquil spell of night, wondering exactly what I was doing and how alone I was feeling. I thought about making a phone call to someone, but I could not think of who to call, so I sat like that, alone, thinking, until the entire room was filled with light. There was one thing, one thing, I kept saying over and over again in my mind: Margaret, I never meant to make you cry.

A STRANGE EPISODE OF *AQUA VOYAGE*

1

A strange episode of *Aqua Voyage* was on the other night, around four o'clock in the morning, and I caught it because I was up all night preparing for a colonoscopy. *Aqua Voyage* was a science fiction show from the seventies that followed a group of underwater explorers who, in each episode, usually discovered a legion of rubber-faced mermaid men or perhaps a very intelligent jellyfish civilization intent on remaining secret. Their ship was called the *Neptune.* Ring a bell? I had seen most of the episodes as a kid. The show was on right after *The Blind Outlaw,* with whisker-faced Brad Burdick, the blind gunman all in black. They were both on right after that show *Manimal,* which didn't run too long.

2

The episode was named "Chapter 18: The Aqua Voyagers Meet the Gill Women of Mars." I didn't think I ever saw it, so I stayed up and watched. Also, the Go

Lightly, the fluid you have to drink a gallon of the night before the colon job, was still working its way through me, but horribly. I was running to the toilet every ten minutes, and what appeared seemed to be exactly what I had drunk moments before—a clear, tasteless fluid—and the pointlessness of it all was very upsetting. In the other room, my wife was sound asleep, already warm and tender and snoring, and each time I heard her breathe, I felt my hands clench with frustration and heat. I sat on the dull gray couch in front of the TV, watching as the silent blue light of the sun began to become less and less ordinary.

3

In the episode, Shark Hansen, the handsome, blond-haired captain, sleek and square chinned in his black and gold jumpsuit, had fallen under the spell of the Gill Women, who were actually from Mars but so, so beautiful, with their long narrow necks and very light blond hair that was as straight as the worried lines of your worried heart. With their powdery blue eye shadow and webbed hands, they were perfect female specimens, except for the pinkish beige gills on their necks. They had come to Earth to take it over, but their ship had crashed into the ocean, and they had been living underwater for hundreds of years, waiting, waiting, waiting. The crew of the *Neptune* had saved them from their watery prison, only to discover the Gill Women still had very dastardly plans for Earth. And with Captain Shark Hansen under the mind-control spell of the lovely Gill Women, it looked like there might be real trouble for the world above the sea—if I could calm my bowels to watch it all, which I could not, unfortunately.

4

The episode, or as much as I saw of it, was a decent one. There was a brutal fight scene with Biff Man-o'-War, the square-headed *Neptune* security chief, who, which I had forgotten, was played by Hal Landon, the former all-star linebacker of the Pittsburgh Steelers. Biff got flattened by the Gill Women, very demure in their blue pastel skirts and black go-go boots that reached up some of the most perilous legs I've ever seen. These gals did these very furious spinning kicks and left Biff in the jettison tube to be torpedoed at the first human warship they came across. Also, Dr. Fathom, the whiny, lily-livered marine biologist, played by British actor Niles Evans, was in top cowardly form, hiding in his lab as the rest of the ship was under attack, muttering, "Oh, my stars, my heavenly stars," until the Gill Women found him, stripped him, and shoved him in a tank with an evil psychic shark the crew had captured a couple of episodes back, or so I presumed. All the underwater imagery was not lost on me, and each time I gave the toilet a flush, I imagined myself somehow escaping with the tide, all the way out to sea.

5

I do not know if I am dying. In a simple way, everybody is constantly and consistently dying, and by that I mean we are getting closer to our own appointed deaths. But most of us do it silently or without much evidence that it is truly happening. If I am dying, I am dying in a very obvious, very dramatic way. I am defecating with such frequency that I must surely have ruptured something. I am bleeding from a place I thought it was impossible to bleed from, my rectum, and I have lost thirty pounds, ten of which I needed to lose anyway. My skin is now as white as a French maid's, and I have been put on leave from work. I have not slept a full night in weeks, because of my frequent need to evacuate, and my wife has taken on the darling, sad, robust look of a war widow in an old copy of *Life* magazine. In two weeks, then a month, then three months' time, I have had many strangers discuss my posterior, from doctors to lab technicians to my neighbors and family and friends. *It could be colitis. It could be Crohn's disease. Is there a history of colon cancer? Yes? Do you have HIV? Are you diabetic?* Each trip to the doctor is a reminder of how completely meaningless television and advertising are because nowhere is there any television show or ad campaign dealing with this.

6

"Hello, dear, how is your rectal bleeding?"

"Just swell, dear! After I took one dose of Happy Colon, I am feeling great."

7

In the middle of the night for months now, I wander around the apartment like a conscience-stricken thief, dragging my feet and mumbling. All is not well in the dark, fine reaches of me.

8

At the end of the episode, the *Neptune* has been taken over. Captain Shark Hansen has laid down his gun and is kissing the feet of the Gill Women queen;

security chief Biff Man-o'-War is trapped in the jettison tube; Dr. Fathom is ensnared in a tank with a two-ton psychic shark; dozens of nameless *Neptune* crew extras have been murdered; and the only one left is Ensign Bobbie Jo Coral, the only female officer, a bubbly brunette with an alluring bob haircut, always in a red jumpsuit, cut to fit so tight that you wonder how she breathed in real life. Bobbie Jo is hiding in an air vent, and the Gill Women are looking all over the ship for her. I get up to run to the toilet, do my business, and when I come back, the show is almost over. The crew has been freed, everyone is safe, and everyone is congratulating Ensign Bobbie Jo on a "job well done." The cable channel the episode was being shown on begins running a marathon infomercial about some fantastic miracle food processor that can cut your fat in half. I never find out how the Gill Women are defeated, and I think that might be symbolic of something at this moment, though I don't know what it might symbolize exactly—something about being confronted with certain doom and not knowing how to escape or how in this world, the world above the sea, nothing ever goes that easily.

9

I begin flipping through the channels again, and finally, out of boredom, I stop at the adults-only numbers, 107, 108, 109, 110, but they are blocked. I can hear what the porno actors are saying—"Yeah, yeah, ohhhh, yeah" and "How do you like that?"—but there is this wavy white line that disrupts the picture, so all I see is a flash of what might be a bare foot, an elbow, a breast. I flip through these channels for a while, and somehow, suddenly, one of the channels is not distorted, and there is this attractive woman in a pool. The adult movie is definitely from the eighties, what with the blinky synthesizer soundtrack and the strange jump cut editing. The woman is wearing a pink swimsuit and has short brown hair. She's in the pool, doing laps, and then pulls herself out. She's soaking wet, and attractive, and she puts sunglasses on to maintain her attractiveness. At this point a tall blond comes in; she has her hair in a ponytail, and already my heart has dropped its jogging pants. I look over my shoulder toward the bedroom to make sure my wife is asleep, knowing that if she walks in now, there'll be nothing I can say to explain myself. Still, I turn up the volume just a little, just to hear what they're saying, because to be honest, I like the dirty talk. The two ladies are rubbing coconut oil on each other, oohing and aahing, and I'm leaning closer and closer. They begin to undress, hands sliding bikinis down shoulder blades, and then they begin to kiss. The blond starts to go down on the brunette, and I am holding my breath; then the blond looks up and says, "Is that your pool boy?" The brunette takes off her sunglasses, and they both look. This big guy with a brown mustache and a blue pool skimmer comes in. Immediately, the man with the mustache begins to undress, and I lean in even more, but just then, as the man is stripping down to small black underpants, well, he just sits down. He just sits down on a blue vinyl pool chair and, like that, he begins to cry, with his head propped in his hands. The two women go to him, are beside him, holding him, and the brunette asks, "What's wrong, Stan?" The guy says, "I am dying," and the blond kisses the man's forehead. For an instant I am sure they are going to start going at it, but the blond just holds the man, and the brunette lady kisses his forehead and says, "You're going to be okay. You'll get through this." The man says, "I don't think so. I don't think I'm gonna make it." I lean in closer, and the brunette says it again, holding the man very close: "You're going to be fine. You're going to get through this," and the blond lady begins to hug the man, and he begins to cry against her chest. The two ladies just hold the man like that for the rest of the movie, no one doing anything, not even kissing, just holding each other, and I suddenly start to cry, too, so happy that someone else in the whole dark world, someone, some adult movie director somewhere, has been through this before me.

HOW TO SAY GOOD NIGHT

1

Many miracles have happened in our town. At night, in bed, I thank you, God, Jesus, and the Holy Ghost, kissing my pillow, praying until dawn with a big heart and many thanks for what I have seen.

2

My cousin, Rey, was born a ghost. He was born without all of his spine, and the town watched him roll about in his rusty wheelchair, waiting for him to die at any moment. Neither his legs nor his arms ever moved; his mouth and eyelids were the only parts of his body that he could control when he wished. He was just thirteen and had short greasy brown hair that was long in the back, an angular face that was larger than the rest of his small, cramped body, and blue eyes that looked like the sad sockets of the Virgin Mary, staring up at her crucified Christ, in a painting at our church. Rey was supposed to live only a few months after he was born but somehow went on year after year, and his many surgeries,

142

BLUEBIRDS USED TO CROON IN THE CHOIR

rehabilitations, and medical supplies made my aunt Sophie very poor and drove my uncle Sonny into the arms of a rich woman who lived in a big house somewhere in the narrow solitude of the panhandle.

Sophie and my cousin lived together in a small brown house with holes in the roof in which sparrows would perch. It was over in the dusty, open stretch of town where most of the Mexican families lived. As I pushed my cousin along, we would find in the gutter along the streets pressed flowers from recent cotillions, washed-out *lotería* cards, and very guilty-looking knives.

In the summer I would go over and visit Rey, offering to roll him down to the dry wash, where he could listen to the soft-throated songs of different birds. Birds were his only comfort in the world, and I would offer to do so because I had fallen in love with his mother, my aunt, Sophie. Sophie was always barefoot. Her toes were so small, like soft white pearls, and I dreamed of kissing them again and again and again. Also, I would only ever see her wearing a small, thin white slip of a nightgown as she sat behind the screen of the front porch, smoking, or stood in the kitchen, crying and baking bread. Also, her soft red hair, which was loose about her delicate neck, and the small red freckles along the bridge of her nose kept me awake in my bed at night, smoldering, during the heat of July, always praying. I would first pray for forgiveness because I knew what I was doing was sinful, thinking such things, offering to massage her neck—and, truly, I was wounded with guilt so bad that whenever I passed a church I would choke back a heavy brace of tears. And then, alone, beneath my sheets, I would pray that somehow, through my dutiful whispering, God would hear how true my love was for this woman and grant me my wish for history to stop for one moment, and one moment only, in which I would as fast as I could, through the humidity of the dark night, ride my bicycle to my cousin's house, gently creep up the bare wood stairs, past my cousin's room that smelled of rubbing alcohol and bandages, and slowly walk into the lone blue bedroom of my aunt Sophie, where I, on my knees like a young bishop, would bow and with all the pleasure of a drunkard begin kissing her very soft feet. At the time Sophie was only thirty-two. I had turned fifteen.

3

During a walk down to the dry wash one day, my cousin and I heard the clanging of ambulance bells nearby. As quickly as I could, I pushed him in his wheelchair, which, having belonged to our great-grandfather, who had been a wounded Civil War veteran, was so rusty that it squeaked constantly as we ran along. We went down an adjoining street, which we never traveled because it was brown and plain and had very little shade. We saw that a small crowd had gathered about a black coupe that had run into the trunk of a small white birch tree. The hood of the automobile was warped, rising upward now, and smoke poured forth from the engine, which looked as though it had tried to climb out. The ambulance arrived just then, and without any sound, two small girls in matching violet dresses were carried from the front porch of a powder blue house by several men and then carefully lifted into the back of the ambulance. By the time we made it to where everyone had gathered, the ambulance doors were closed and it was already pulling away, its bells starting to clang again, and people began turning to each other and whispering.

"An accident?" I heard a soapy-faced old man ask, removing his gray hat to wipe his sweaty forehead and then replacing it. He nodded and pressed his hand against the very narrow white birch tree.

"The Blanca sisters," a young woman replied, shielding her eyes from the sun and dust from the street. "They were run down. Look here." She pointed to a large gash that had been dug into the thin trunk of the tree. Along the chrome front bumper of the automobile, where it had been dented sharply, were the small round droplets of what I knew to be blood. There was another gruesome mark: a dark patch of dirt and dust growing from beneath the front wheels. It was in the shape of two small angels, arms outspread as if they had been flying when they were struck down. Just then a woman in a yellow dress, with a scarf about her head, fell to her knees and began praying. Others followed, and soon my cousin, Rey, was whispering along, his closed eyelids fluttering.

4

Very soon, people were leaving flowers and photographs of the Blanca sisters beside the birch tree. Then there were several small stuffed animals, then larger ones, the kind you might win at a carnival or a fair. Candles, left in small brown paper bags, burned throughout the night. There would always be a crowd about the spot, and as I pushed Rey down to the dry wash, he would whisper, "Past the tree, past the tree," and we would turn and take our new path down the unpaved brown street.

Many weeks later, the girls were returned to their narrow little blue house, not dead but not quite alive either. Both had been sitting in the only shade of the street that summer day. Dolores, who had been combing the hair of her identical twin, Juana, was struck and then knocked completely from this world. Their ghosts were willing to depart perhaps, but their little hearts went on beating, their pulses the only flicker of movement in their small narrow wrists.

A man by the name of Mendez was the first. A bus driver, he passed by the Blanca house each morning at dawn on his way to work and again late in the evening on his way home. He worked nearly eighteen hours each day. Having been poor his whole life and having made some very bad bets of late, he stopped in front of the small blue house, stared up at the thin blue curtains of the second floor, where he believed the twin girls were quietly asleep, and mumbled a little prayer that went like this: "Father in heaven, take pity on these two girls, and in your wisdom—your wisdom which has put enough food on my table and brought me three beautiful boys and a wife who is as smart as she is lovely, though, yes, a job as night supervisor would be a blessing, a blessing perhaps I do not deserve—please grant that they may get up and walk again someday, or at least grant their parents some kind of end, peace. Perhaps, Father, perhaps just peace for all of us then."

More than a few minutes later, as he strode into the shadows of the open garage of the maintenance pool of the city bus line, his boss, a man named Epsom, gently clapped his hand on Mendez's shoulder and declared, "Mendez, today is your day. You just made night supervisor."

Days later, an elderly woman who suffered horribly from rheumatism was resting against the birch tree as she worked her way home from the market. She found that her left hand, which for the last thirteen years had been nothing more than a fleshy, unyielding hook, gently began to uncurl, each finger growing light and as painless as a feather. She quickly crossed herself, knelt down, closed her eyes, and praised the Blanca sisters over and over again.

More than a few weeks had passed by the time I was pushing Rey along the narrow street and we saw dozens of notices, in both Spanish and English, on very tiny pieces of paper. Tied to the white branches of the birch tree, they declared how prayers had been answered at this spot, wishes made true, reprieves granted. Rey looked up at me, his eyes round and terrified, yet full of hope. He closed his eyes and reached his neck forward, moving awkwardly as he attempted to place his cheek against the white birch tree. He could not, though. So lifting him beneath his armpits as carefully as I could, I allowed him to press his forehead against the soft white bark, biting back his tears, stuttering his prayers. He then settled back in his wheelchair and immediately fell asleep from exhaustion. I stared up at the blue window of the blue house, thought of the two girls, closed my eyes, and placed the cup of my palm against a narrow branch from a low limb, making my terrible wish.

5

Many weeks later, in the middle of the night, a curtain of rain and thunder covered our town, and as I lay in bed, my eyes open, imagining what my aunt Sophie would whisper as I so delicately placed my hands along the very bottom hem of her nightgown and lifted—"Oh, but we shouldn't, we shouldn't. You are a bad boy, a very bad boy"—the phone began to ring. From the sound of my mother's voice on the telephone, the softness of it, like a very sympathetic nun speaking, I knew at once it was my aunt calling, and then for some reason I was overcome with—what? I do not know. Bravery, hope, fear maybe. In only my underwear, I pulled myself from my bed and out through the cellar door. I crept up through the dark into the night, the cool splendor of the heavy rain running along my naked neck and hands and face. Finding my small red bicycle, I began to pedal, howling with laughter as I drove faster and faster. Finally I was turning down their street, toward their small, square house on the corner, the white light in my aunt's kitchen the only light still burning anywhere in the flood of rain. The sound of wind rattling windows and the squeak of the small silver wheels before I threw my bicycle to the ground and ran around to the back door, which was always left unlocked, and saw the shape of my aunt, waiting behind the dark screen. She began calling my name, and it was just as I had dreamed for so long. *It was just as I dreamed,* for there on the clothesline, which ran from one corner of the small yard to the other, was the very thin white nightgown, almost invisible now with the rain, held fast with two wooden clothespins. And the small light in the kitchen declared the bare rounded shoulders of my aunt, standing there naked, not embarrassed, no, but laughing, calling out my name and laughing. The very small, pearl-shaped curve of my aunt's breasts, her tiny belly button, the narrow stretch of the top of one leg appeared, then disappeared, as she shifted in the light, hopping about giddily.

"Be a good boy!" she called. "My slip, my slip, it's out there!" I turned toward the clothesline, then looked back again—my aunt's red hair looking so red, lit from behind, and a small path of freckles running along the top of her bare chest. I could not move. My heart was beating so hard, and my hands were shaking at the wrists.

"Be a good boy now! Be good! Yes, hurry!" she called. Then, opening the back door just enough to place her head out, she shouted, "Hurry, it is Reynaldo! He has begun kicking!"

I turned and walked on the ground that rose like mountaintops beneath my bare feet, gently pulling the pins from the straps of the slip, holding the wet fabric in my hands, carrying it like an armful of gold toward the back door, this most precious set of stitches, this, the only border to my most beautiful imaginings, and at the very last moment, I could walk no farther. I was standing there, almost naked myself, staring at her, the shape of her through the screen so close, and yet I couldn't move forward. She kept on giggling, her laugh not like a woman's laugh but like a schoolgirl's. "Be a good boy now. You must hurry!" But I could not walk forward, so she stepped out from behind the screen door, her bare shoulders, her stomach, the mound of her pubic hair, coming forward, closer, closer, slowly inching into the rain, and her hair becoming wet and dark, her bare feet glistening. I began to run, overcome with shame or fear again, perhaps, and she began to laugh, calling out, "You are a bad boy, a very bad boy!" as she chased me about the yard and then, along the side of the house, catching me when I fell against the fence, her bare hand on my chest as she laughed and finally tugged the gown from my hands.

WOMEN I HAVE MADE CRY

1

Birdie McCoy is a girl I make cry in third grade. When I do it, I doom myself forever. In the woods behind the elementary school, blue bows in her brown hair, her face red from a race, she is given a yellow ribbon for winning. I say, out of breath, "Who's going to marry an ugly girl like you?" and she begins to cry quietly, for being faster than me, smarter, so small, so pretty. As she cups her hands over her eyes, I fall in love for the first time. Many years later I realize it is there, that moment, that dooms me forever. I fall in love with a woman as soon as she begins crying, which always, always occurs at the end of everything.

2

Outside a white chapel in Deermont, awaiting a relation's wedding, I am holding hands with my cousin, Elizabeth Montgomery. We are both only ten years of age. I have a clip-on tie, and her ladylike gloves are folded neatly in her lap. She weeps when I tell her that, no matter what, we can't be married.

3

On a sofa, in her white collegiate sweater, Patsy McGiness from my psych class hisses through her teeth. I don't remember why, only the sound she makes, hissing and blinking her eyes, which are soft and wet and make me want to kiss her when before there was nothing between us, nothing.

4

In New York, years later, dating a soap star, the first woman I ever moved in with, who I imagined was the one. A darling redhead, in person she could make you whistle "The Star-Spangled Banner" when she winked. In real life, though, her name was plain—Debbie, short for Debra Ann—and she told me this one Sunday morning while I was cooking her pancakes at her place. She had introduced herself to me a few weeks before as Blythe. I had met her at a friend's engagement party, at which she had purposefully outshined the bride-to-be. During the wedding ceremony itself, she kept arranging and rearranging the bride's white lacy train and veil. I saw it as a cry for attention or just plain jealousy maybe. In intimate moments, though, I held the name Blythe on my lips, so when she told me the truth weeks later, I wrote her real name in maple syrup on a stack of silver dollars and served it to her like that: DEBBIE ANN. She ate them, bashfully, and looked at me with a look like love, with tears in her eyes, tears in her eyes just like that, because of the secret we were then sharing. I saw the tears and fell for her, worse than any woman I have met, worse and very immediately.

During the title sequence of the soap she was on, her name appeared as Blythe Lynn just as she winked and flipped her hair for the camera. She was on *The Young and the Restless* for almost six years, I think. She videotaped her own show every day while she was there working, and I went over to her place with some takeout and we watched it together every night. She told me strange secrets about her costars. "That guy shaves all of his body hair," she said as she pointed to some handsome buck with an eye patch, dashing, calculating a hostile takeover in a white silk robe. "That one, that lady beside him, is forty-two."

"She looks like she's twenty," I said.

"Everything on her is plastic." She smiled knowingly, her feet in my lap as a simple message that she intended to have them massaged, and if I didn't, there would be no intimacy later. "Now that guy, the one with the big chin, he stole a pair of my stockings from the dressing room the other day."

On the show she played a sixteen-year-old nymph named Donna Brandenmeyer whose primary purpose was to seduce the older men of the cast, mostly millionaires, I guess. I don't think she ever wore anything other than a delicious private school uniform: plaid skirt, kneesocks, white blouse, and even pink barrettes in her hair. Once or twice she brought the outfit home, and I nearly ruined it with my enthusiasm. In one particular scene from the show, which I remember very clearly, because, well, it was pretty arousing, Donna commanded a handsome older gent with white hair and a perfect mustache to get down on his knees and crawl across a broken bottle of champagne to get to her. The man nodded and dropped to his knees, and Donna started laughing and unbuttoning her blouse, letting it fall to her feet. She was always doing that on the show, unbuttoning her blouse or skirt or dress, and the camera switched to a shot of her from behind and poof! The dress dropped, and you got a clear shot of Debbie's or Blythe's or Donna's bare back, which was not too tan or too white but it was soft—you could see how soft and muscular it was even on TV. For a while I was pretty sure the attraction between us was her ability to cry for no real reason, on cue, even, but perhaps it was also that she played a sixteen-year-old vamp and sometimes slipped into the role for me. At a restaurant or on the couch, watching that day's tape, she would unbutton her top and let it fall off her shoulders, and in her very innocent, very dumb high school girl voice she'd say, "Look. Look what's happened here to my top. Well, how clumsy." Other times, sitting by the window, she would practice her crying, which forced me to lift her into my arms so that I could carry her off into bed while she was still weeping.

One night Debbie brought home the next week's script, and in it were two sets of lines, one highlighted in blue, one highlighted in red. "What goes on here?" I asked.

"I'm playing my own evil twin," she said, and that was pretty much the beginning of the end for us, I guess. The evil twin was even more of a vamp, and on the show she messed up Donna's engagement to Rick, the down-and-out pool guy who happened to save Donna's life after she had taken an unhealthy dose of sleeping pills and tried to end it all in the hot tub by drowning. Rick pulled her out, and they fell in love—just on the show, or at least that's the way I wanted to think of it. Soon enough the evil twin, Connie, showed up and slept with nearly all the male characters, including Rick, the beloved, and, well, I can't figure out who I liked better out of all of them: Debbie, who wrote YOU LOVE ME with her fingertip on my bare chest and cried or was always on the verge of crying; Blythe, who laughed extra loud at the cast parties and then whispered something dirty to me; Donna, who might have had something decent about her if she had only believed in love and stayed with a good fellow like Rick; or Connie, who was bad news but kind of every man's fantasy, or at least my kind of fantasy at that time.

One night while we were sitting on the couch and watching the show from the day before, in which some tanned dude named Brock in one of those puffy white pirate-type shirts was making out with Debbie/Blythe/Donna/Connie, I looked over at her, and she was mouthing her own lines to herself. I said, "Hey, does that ever get you turned on? Making out with all those different guys?"

Debbie just rolled her eyes and then pushed up against me and said, "Why? Does it turn you on, seeing me make out with some other guy?"

I didn't want to think about that, so I said, "Nope. I can safely say that it doesn't turn me on in the least."

"Then, no. If it doesn't turn you on, it doesn't turn me on."

"Okay, well, do those actors ever, you know, get turned on?"

"That guy, the guy who plays Rick, told me that he fantasizes about me all the time."

"Wait. He told you that, or his character on the show said that?"

"Him. The actor."

"Well, that's great," I said. "Doesn't he know we're dating?"

"He plays Rick, for God's sake. He can have any woman he wants."

"Except you," I said.

"He could probably have me, too, if he tried," she said, winking at me and laughing.

"So who are you being right now?" I asked, pushing her feet off me.

"What?" she asked.

"I mean, who are you being right now?"

Outside, it had begun snowing very quietly. Inside the apartment, there was no sound except the sound of Donna on TV laughing, arguing with a bluescreen Connie, herself, and Debbie beside me, breathing kind of funny.

"I don't know who I'm being," she said, and that was it. She started crying. I didn't know if they were stage tears or not. I could never tell anyway. Outside, the whole world was dark and quiet, and I imagined someone very far away shouting through a megaphone, "That's a wrap," and the next thing I knew, I had invented a reason to leave and was already going.

5

Over the phone, Molly Anders cried the way she does, making one quick sound like a gulp of air, when I said that since I was away at college now, we shouldn't remain exclusive, we should start dating other people. I heard her make the sound, and we hung up quickly. My heart was pounding. I dialed her number again, but it only went on ringing.

6

Months before she moved away to have a baby, I teased Emily Bourke, a girl I knew, at a high school football game about her putting on weight. She cocked her head, bit her lip, and her brown eyes got glossy; then she turned and climbed down from the bleachers. I stood up to say something but could only watch her leave.

7

In fifth grade, while I was daydreaming about small towns on the moon, my mother went to the car wash every day to cry and to get a wax and sealant treatment. She was, like every other woman in the neighborhood, going through a divorce. It was her second already. She didn't want me to know what was going on, and I didn't notice until a huge chunk of paint was chipped off the minivan on the passenger side and two antennas on the front end were snapped. She went to the White Glove Car Wash around the corner from us, turned the radio station to soft rock classics, and while Karen Carpenter crooned gently, my mother pulled inside the automated car wash and screamed and cried tears so infinitely small that one dab of wadded-up tissue from her purse easily hid her shame. Then she returned home and finished doing my laundry and the laundry of her soon-to-be-second ex-husband.

8

In bed, the worst mistake I ever made was with an amateur ice-skater named Gail. I made her acquaintance in college, and when the incident happened, she was in a traveling company like the Ice Capades but of a lower caliber, for athletes who were not Ice Capades material. I think the company was called the North American Ice Ballet. She came to town around Christmastime and called me up, saying she didn't know anybody in town and it was Christmas and she was lonely and her company was doing *The Nutcracker* on ice and would I like to come to see it. Sure, I said, and she said she was in the chorus of soldiers, not a starring role but not so bad, what with all the major roles being reserved for "trampy women and has-been effeminate men" anyway. She sent me tickets at work, and I went to the show. I am not sure if I even saw her perform because of all the costumes and everything, but I brought her flowers, which someone had sent to work but never claimed, and later we went to the hotel where she was staying. She put on the cable TV, and I watched the news while she slipped into the bathroom. She came out and turned off the lights, and from the get-go, it was trouble. She was a talker, and while I was trying to get on with unbuttoning her clothing, she began telling me about how a major skating agent had a vested interest in her. She was very ticklish as well. When I did something that tickled her, she kind of barked, like a seal, and it killed the mood for me instantly. Then, well, as we were in the middle of it, she kind of, well, grabbed her own breasts, the way women do in porno movies, but in real life, well, it makes me laugh immediately. She got red in the face and became kind of stiff to let me know I hurt her feelings, and, well, it ended very badly. Eventually, I came, and as a joke, I don't know, I gave her a high five, just to break the tension, and when I looked over my shoulder, she said, "This is not how I wanted this to go at all. I did not even want to sleep with you," and she was holding herself and crying.

In junior high there was this girl that I had a terrible crush on, Amanda Bradley. She sat directly behind me, and I asked her out on a date every day at twelve o'clock when the lunch bell rang. I turned around in my seat, looked at her, and said, "Amanda, will you go out with me?" Everybody in the class laughed, and Amanda's small, freckled, pink face got red. She looked down and was afraid to say a word, because she was so kind, so gentle, so polite that she even gave me a valentine that year that said, "I think we can be great friends." Every day at twelve o'clock she looked down at her perfect peanut butter and jelly sandwich, with the crust cut off and sliced in four perfect squares, and simply shook her head no sadly. It went on like this every day for weeks, then months. Every day I saw her face go from pleasant pink to squeamish green the closer the second hand rose to the top of the clock, and as the bell shuddered in the air, I turned and before I even asked, she, out of pity, perhaps disgust, already had her head down, shaking it no, no, no and eventually crying.

A stewardess, a girl at Tastee Freeze, and our school nurse. Somehow I say the wrong thing, but exactly.

Now

In your apartment, you are listening to the Smiths, and I make some bad comment and touch your skirt and go to undo the button of your blouse. You look up, dreamy, all blue eyes, and say, "You're never going to want to have kids, are you?"

"Not on purpose, anyway," I say, still trying to undo your top.

"For real?"

"Yes, for real. There's enough goddamn people as it is. The best thing I can do is just try to take care of myself." And I keep at it, and you just lay there, and in the middle of my kissing your neck, you say, very softly, very quietly, "You're never gonna change," which isn't a statement so much as a realization, and I say, "I don't want to change. Change is for people who get it wrong."

I am joking, but you aren't, and after I say it, the guy, the singer in the Smiths, whines something loudly. You have your face turned and I can hear you breathing hard, and I see the red in your cheeks and you are about to cry, you are about to cry, but you don't, you don't sputter or weep or make a sound, and I don't know what to do, because any other girl in the world would have stormed out already or told me to leave, and with anyone else I would have been halfway down the street, but there you are, and we are on your sofa, and I think, What do we do now? because this has never happened before, and you turn and face me, and you seem to be asking me something with your eyes, something very important like, *Would you like to be an adult in love now? Would you like to give that a try?* and all I can answer is, *More than anything in the world, yes, yes, I would like to try.*

A TOWN OF NIGHT

Once night arrived, it wouldn't leave. It came at dusk on time, and when it should have been gone, it refused to secede. It settled in the grit of our bones and made us believe what we wanted to believe, which, in the empty gristle of our heads, added up to something a little less than larceny.

Our own Hal Parkins, from the mill, union brother-in-arms, had been driving alone along Route 41 and had caught sight of the century-old ghosts of the lost Mexican army, who were known to march from the spot near the piney woods where they had been slaughtered by the Illinois volunteer militia to the place where they had dropped dead in a Baptist cemetery, which stands in the same spot to this day, not minding that the Baptist church burned down over thirty years ago at the hands of the Klan. Well, Hal Parkins had been drinking to weld his evil pride shut, on account of his wife taking leave with a journeyman from our own mill, a fellow named Ricky, who happened to work the same spot on the line as Hal during the day shift, which led everyone to believe that while Hal was wringing his hands at work, Ricky was at home in Hal's own place, and then they would switch, and it went on a while like that, without Hal ever knowing the trade he was making. Well, when Hal's rum-soaked eyes caught sight of the soldiers crossing Route 41, blood on their faces and the sad profundity of death bundled with tourniquets in their severed arms, he yanked the truck's steering wheel to the far right and spun off the road, finally looking up. It must have been like staring into an antique mirror of your own end, because there was the well-meaning iron net fence and, beyond that, our town's three generators, humming there silently without repentance. Before he could jump, his truck barreled through the soft wire and conduit and condensers, lighting up the border sky like a Mexican hero's holiday, all silver and white and full of sad fire. Within a minute the sky was a show of smoke. In another minute, Hal had faded into some kind of slow disintegration, and our whole town was quiet and dark.

In an hour or two, mostly everyone had heard what had happened. When all the lights went out, my brother, Bill, and I were at the Last Call, which was the bar we favored around there. The bartender, Trudie, decided it was best to send everyone home early, lonely or not. We were still sitting in my brother's truck in the parking lot, drinking from a bottle of Maker's Mark, when that loudmouth Bartlett came around and started spouting about how our poor fellow union brother-in-arms, Hal Parkins, was dust to dust. Then he mentioned that there would be no power for at least two days, three on the outside, considering the job old Hal had done. Immediately, my brother and I put the bottle down and began thinking that the mill would definitely be closed and we wouldn't have to work the next few days for sure, which didn't mean anything, because there would be nothing to do in town now anyway. The bowling alley, the movie house, and the Last Call would all be closed, definitely. Then we began to think that at least there was nothing in our refrigerator that would spoil because we didn't have nothing in our refrigerator in the first place. But then Bill said that since we didn't have any food, we were in trouble, because no one would be serving any anywhere else, probably. And then we passed the bottle between us and began to think seriously. We could see the candles slowly being lit in the windows of the houses along the street, and it was like thoughts slowly taking shape in our own evil brains. We began to think that maybe this was it, maybe this was our opportunity to do what we had dreamed of for so long, which was to steal the mare we were always eyeing.

The horse my brother and I had been watching was white and known to predict the future, no lie. It had a soft beige mouth and eyes that were nearly pink. It was about twenty years old, twenty-five at the most, and belonged to an old woman who lived down the road. G. HUZEL it read on the mailbox, which was gray wood. The farm was crumbling around her like a coffin. The white mare would trot along its broken fence posts and stare out at me and my brother as we drove past to work at the mill, and the horse's soft yellow mane would whip just out of reach of our hands.

The horse had predicted several important events, which more than proved its abilities to us. It had predicted the president's trip to Dallas in 1963 and the following tragedies. The whole town knew before anyone what was going to happen, because the old woman had flown her flag at half-mast for weeks before that November day, and the afternoon the shot was fired, the flag had been pulled from its post, almost as if by the ghost itself. When the town flooded five years back, everyone looked to the old woman to see how long it would last, and when she began to hang her laundry out in the yard days before the waters withdrew, we all knew the predicament would soon pass.

The way she worked was like this: She was some kind of Scandinavian, and she would go out to the barn every morning and sing some Scandinavian tune. It would move the white horse so much that the beast would begin to cry, and if the tears fell in one silver bucket, it meant one thing, and if the tears fell in another, it meant something else. So she would sing to it and ask questions, and you could go to the old woman and give her five dollars and ask her a question. She'd take you out to the barn and do it exactly as I'm telling you now, which my brother and I had done when our own mother left us. Our father was already gone, and we didn't know what we had done wrong to deserve any of the meanness we had been wrestling with. So now my brother and I both figured that with the blackout and all, we could steal that horse, sell it over the border in Matamoros, Mexico, and make enough money not to have to ever come back to town for nothing, which had been my dream for so long.

We would need pistols, Bill decided. I don't know why, but we were pretty sure pistols would be a good thing to have. We would have to steal those, too, I guessed. There was an old fellow who sold firearms in town, and if he wasn't open and selling, we would have to break in there, too, but Bill and I agreed that having a pistol would be worth it. So that night, when the whole town was dim and dark, we pulled out of the Last Call's parking lot, drove down two streets and over one, parked the truck, and climbed out. We were officially engaging in some very felonious activities, prowling around a gun shop in the middle of the night during a blackout and all. It was downright evil, I think now. Bill tried the back door, and I just stood there watching. "Shit," he whispered. "It's locked." Like he expected the door to be any other way.

I nodded and started wondering how much that mare might fetch in old Mex.

Bill shook the lock again, clanging around, and a candle was lit in the room above the shop. As it turned out, the man who sold the guns lived above the shop, and when he heard us snooping around, he called out from his window and started hollering at us.

"Whatcha snooping around for? We're closed." The old fellow's face was like burlap and crowned with a silver patch of hair alongside his ears.

"We weren't sure you might be open, with the power out and all," Bill shouted back. "You know, people might like to be armed."

"Well, we're closed just the same," the old man shouted back. "Now clear out."

"All right, old-timer, no need to get rowdy."

The light blew out above the shop, and Bill and I walked back over to his truck.

"So now what?" I asked.

"We can't go back there now. He's expecting us."

"Well, maybe we don't need a pistol anyway," I said.

"It doesn't make sense not to have one. You don't know what might happen. It's a tool of intimidation. What if that lady out there gives us trouble?"

"What? You gonna shoot her?" I asked, shaking my head.

"No. I mean, you might need a gun to scare her and all."

"I guess. Couldn't we just use something else then?"

"Like what?" he asked.

"I dunno. Like a knife or a pipe."

"Shit, brother, you're strictly amateur, huh?" And again I began to wonder what a prizewinning mare like that might be worth, what it might be able to get us, I mean, like a decent place or some cash that we could double at some blackjack tables maybe. I sat quietly thinking in the dark as my brother circled the gun shop in the truck once, then got tired and gave up.

"Tomorrow night," Bill said.

"Tomorrow night then. All right."

The horse had no intention of being stolen, as I saw it. I was pretty sure. We drove past the farm twice the next day to make sure it was still there and in healthy condition, and on the second time past, Bill honked at the thing as it was running along the worn wood fence and whistled, "Hey, girl!" The horse just ignored us and ran into a grove of pear trees, disappearing in the perfumed breeze like a dream. Bill pulled over on the side of the road and stared at the gray slant-board house.

"I don't see anyone moving around out there," Bill said, nodding to himself maybe.

"She might be inside sleeping," I said back. "It's hot, you know. She ain't gonna be out in the sun now or anything."

"I guess."

Bill eyed the house, studying it with a stern look, curling his lips together tightly.

"So how are we gonna steal it then? You gonna ride it out of town or what?" I asked.

"Shit, brother," Bill said, and I noticed this was the second time he had said this to me in two days. "There's a horse trailer out there by the house, see. We just hook up the trailer, put the horse inside, and drive away." He turned the wheel a little to straighten it out on the road and laughed. "It'll be easy—easier than any of your old girlfriends, buddy."

"My old girlfriends? Shit. No girl of *mine* ever ran around."

"That's because everyone came to them," my brother said with a snicker.

Then I got sore and stopped laughing and for spite said, "Deirdre Shelton."

After I said it, I wished I hadn't, because Bill didn't make a sound. Somehow, though, I could hear his heart breaking up, which I imagined was like a tiny candle being blown out. We sat in his truck in silence for a few minutes more, staring at the old lady's farm, and then we took off. Afterward, we circled town, then the block of the gun shop, and then Bill got out. In a minute he climbed back in without a word, and like a threat, he handed me a pistol in a small wood box.

As it was, the town was getting along fine without power. The firemen had opened a fireplug for kids to play in, and some council people were going around saying that the power would be back on tomorrow. Bill didn't say a word to me except, "Pack your shit," which wasn't hard, because all I had were some clothes that fit in a paper bag and some old baseball cards, which I had spent a lot of time organizing in a black album that said FAMILY PHOTOS, which was a gas, because no one in my family had ever done anything half as decent as playing professional baseball like Sandy Koufax. I sat in front of the window and watched as the whole world began to get dark. I watched some kids lighting candles inside small brown paper bags along the street. I got restless waiting, so I decided to go for a walk. No one was outside. It was like a ghost town from the movies. There was the sound of a dog barking, and that was it. It was nice. Some fireflies were scattered around. I got to thinking about what we were going to do, and I got sad. I don't know. I kept thinking of that old woman going out to the barn and seeing her horse gone and how it might be like we had stolen her heart, so I tried not to think about it. I headed back and stopped to watch a family sitting around a candle in the kitchen eating hot dogs, and then I hid in some bushes, because I thought one of them had seen me. Then I went back to our place to see if Bill was ready.

He was staring out the window and, I dunno, I was afraid to ask, but he was sitting in the chair and crying for some reason.

"Are you ready?" I asked.

"Yes," he said.

I could see that the track of tears along his face had made its way to his shirt, which meant he must've been crying for some time.

"I'll get my things," I said and went and got my family album.

A moment before we got in the truck, Bill said, "Deirdre Shelton is getting married."

I looked around. The whole town was now completely dark. Well, not completely. There was some flicker of candlelight behind the curtains of a few houses, but that was it. I looked at the houses and then at my brother and said, "What? Who said that?"

"That loudmouth Bartlett said Deirdre is getting married. Next week."

"Jesus," I said, and I meant it this time. Deirdre was the main reason Bill was so mean and was now living with me. They had been engaged for six years while my brother was in the navy, and when he got a dishonorable discharge and came back home, Deirdre acted like those six years hadn't meant a thing. As it was, she had been catting around, and maybe as his brother I ought to have warned him, but a fool is the fellow who gets involved in someone else's mistakes of love, or so a song by Patsy Cline or some nice lady like that on the jukebox at the Last Call declares, and I'm not one strong enough to doubt it.

"Well then, her getting married is just one more reason to do this," I said.

"I ain't sore she's getting married," he whispered, switching on the headlights. "I'm just sore it ain't to me," and that was the last thing he said before we drove from the shanty we rented, along Faber Road, and up to the gates of the old lady's place.

A chain connected the gates, but it wasn't locked with anything. Bill hopped out, unlooped the chain, and swung the gates open as gently as you please. Bill got back in the truck, started up the little gray road, and switched the headlights off.

"What's to keep her from calling the police?" I asked suddenly. "Just because the power ain't working doesn't mean the phone is down."

Bill just shook his head and nodded at me. The look was supposed to mean something, but I didn't like it, so I said, "Oh, no, Bill, I'd rather wrestle that horse than do something like that."

"Shit, brother," he said again. "I'm giving you the easy job. Just take the gun and flash it around." He dug under the seat and handed me the small wood box.

"Open it," he said.

"I don't wanna open it," I said back.

"Go on and open it," he grunted, and so I did. There was this old-fashioned pistol sitting there in my hands. It had to be ninety-three million years old. One part of it was stuck together with string and wire, and another part was taped. The trigger was shaky and seemed ready to fall out.

"What am I supposed to do with this?" I whispered.

"Make sure she doesn't call the cops."

"It isn't even loaded," I said.

"Jesus. It was the only one I could afford, you know. Use your goddamn imagination or something." He shoved me again, left the truck running, and climbed out. He winked at me and headed toward the barn. I climbed out and just stood there, staring at the house that was strung together with hunks of nail and shingle. It looked ready to fall in on itself. I watched the windows to see if anyone was moving inside, and it looked like the coast was clear. I headed around back, looking for where the only door might be, and decided I ought to get rid of the gun. I put it behind a little green bush and crept farther around, finding a very shadowy spot. I held my breath in the dark. I could hear Bill hooking up the horse trailer to the truck, the sound of the engine running, and the blossoms from the pear trees rising and falling in the night air, like kisses being mailed all around me. I heard Bill open the back gate of the trailer and the sound of his steps as he wandered into the barn.

I pressed my face up against the glass of the back door and stared inside.

Someone was in there moving, but very slowly. I took a step back and saw it was the old woman, and she was reaching for the phone. My mouth went all dry suddenly, and she must've heard me move because she stopped where she was and just sat there with the receiver in her hand. I was just standing there, too, shaking my head, begging, pleading, without saying a word. She was begging and pleading back in her own way, her small eyes turning blue with tears, her lips tight in a small pink O, and her hands shaking so clearly.

There we were, two humans, begging and pleading and praying to each other not to do the thing each of us must've feared. So we didn't. We just stood there like two old lovers, maybe, or like I was an artist studying her for a painting or she was the painter and I was the subject, which would be "What a Criminal Is," maybe. The old lady's face was smooth and white and sad, not scared but sad, and she was crying. I was just standing there. Then the woman did the darnedest thing. In the middle of it all, she just opened her mouth and began to sing.

The voice was old and wispy, like the sound you'd imagine coming from the door of that worn-out house, and it was so gentle, so light that I felt my lips lifting themselves from my teeth in a smile. Then I shook that loose in time, spun around quickly, and ran to get back in the truck. But when I came across from the side of the house, my brother was nowhere to be found. The trailer hadn't even been hooked up. I started to panic, and I could feel my face turning red. I ran straight through the barn doors, and there was Bill, my lousy brother. He was on his knees beside the white horse and crying into his hands. Then he lifted his head, looked right at me, and said, "She's pregnant. Deirdre Shelton's pregnant with some fella's baby, goddamn it." He kicked over one of the silver buckets and kept on crying. Afterward, when we were on the interstate and just about to cross into old Mex, my brother and I still hadn't said a thing.

ASTRONAUT OF THE YEAR

10

The Astronaut of the Year is unhappy. We do not know why. He has just received a national award and still wears the foggy space helmet. He is all knotted white eyebrows and gritted teeth, and for some reason he is shouting. In the back of the complimentary shuttle car, he demands that we immediately take him to a bar where there will be many young women. These are his words exactly: "many young women." We do not expect him to say words like that because he is wearing a space helmet and has wrinkly hands and a big gold medal pinned to his chest. To us he looks precisely like a grandfather who has come back from the dead. He looks proud and taciturn and sad, like an angel in his silver Mylar military uniform — out of place in our world entirely. Above the pressed collar and beneath the glass helmet he is all chin. His skin is bright liver spots and acres of wrinkles. He is in the backseat of the Celebration Corporation's biggest and best shuttle car, a mondo-size silver Cadillac DeVille — also available for weddings, bar mitzvahs, and corporate events—and his arms are folded over the aforementioned big gold medal. He announces that he will jump out of the car if we do not obey his wishes this very instant. We speak up and say we know a few places. We say we can try to help him meet a few ladies.

9

The Astronaut of the Year does have a first name and a last name. Together, they are Mr. Chet Aston. They are on the yellow paperwork of the shuttle car order, Celebration Corporation Celebrity Escort 212, sitting silently beside us on the front passenger seat. We do not dare speak to the astronaut using either name. It is because we recognize his face from history books, newspapers, films, posters, place mats, coffee cups, T-shirts, buttons, baseball hats, ceramic garlic holders, and welcome mats. The man's features tell us all about humanity's conquest of the vast expanse of outer space and our need to explore and accept the dark, unshiny, and very lonely voids within all of us. We remember wondering what he must have felt like up there, alone, quiet, floating. We remember wondering what he was thinking. We realize he has been to a place we will never, could never even begin to understand. In this he is almost like a victim turned celebrity. We decide to simply refer to him as "sir" when we ask him if he is sure he does not want to go on to the reception as planned. "People are expecting you there, probably, sir," we say.

The Astronaut of the Year says, "I've been into space thirteen times." Then he adds, very angrily, "You. You are all like very little ants to me."

The Astronaut of the Year does not seem to notice that we do not usually do well with angry people. We are slightly self-medicated and trying not to enter a reactionary shame spiral of violence. God knows, we are trying. We are really only me, just me, the driver, up front, alone. My name? Brian, but we have been trained to always refer to ourselves as "we," in deference to the collective of the Celebration Corporation, as a sign of our sense of corporate oneness and cohesion, and also as a psychological device to keep ourselves as drivers from feeling isolated and lonely, as best judged in the following important customer-based interactions: "We at Celebration Corporation want to thank you for riding with us today, sir," or "We at Celebration Corporation had a lovely time serving you today, sir," or "We at Celebration Corporation would appreciate it if you waited until your next stop to partake of illegal substances, sir."

We are also me—Brian—and the photograph of my ex-girlfriend, Jean, which I have been carrying everywhere recently. It is the only photo I have of a girl who was a catalog model for clothing for petite and height-challenged women, and it is not even actually a photo but a picture torn from one of her ads, in which she is standing beside a miniature brown pony, modeling a lovely miniature wedding dress. In the ad there are tiny stars in her eyes, and her brown hair is threaded with small white flowers. She is feeding the pony a sugar cube from the palm of her hand and laughing the way I had imagined her laughing when we actually got married. But like the miniature pony, she has moved on to greener pastures now, having gotten the role of a lifetime playing the title character on a syndicated television series, *World's Tallest Man Marries World's Shortest Woman,* which critics and audiences alike have been thoroughly enjoying. In the end, the we, the torn catalog picture of Jean and me, have still been getting along okay and enjoying each other's company, working together, driving the shuttle car, which the real Jean was never interested in doing, and also going to the park, restaurants, and movies, which Jean was always loath to do because of her very obvious and diminutive size. We miss the real Jean but not her constant complaining about "heightists" and a culture obsessed with celebrity perfection, which, strangely enough, she is now somehow part of, we guess. We miss the real Jean but not the way she could make us feel worse than when we were lonely. We remember today is our eleven-month anniversary but forget if it is the anniversary of the paper Jean or the real Jean. We do not really care. To us, eleven months either way is still an accomplishment. It is still something.

7

The Astronaut of the Year spits at us suddenly as we are considering the real Jean. We decide maybe it is best if the astronaut does not go on to the reception at all. We cruise around for a while, hoping again that he will change his mind. But he does not. He curses the people who are smiling at him as we drive past. He calls us a ninny. He threatens us with bodily harm. We take deep breaths and try to forget how easy it would be to smash an old man's windpipe. We remember, after all, who the old man is. We stare at the clipping of Jean sitting in our lap and try to be happy, peaceful, calm, understanding. We circle through the city, slowly, slowly, creating great invisible figure eights until the Astronaut of the Year is asleep in the backseat. We turn on the radio and sing a love song to the photo of Jean, remembering our kissing on the beach at dawn, though we had never been to the beach. We check the paperwork and see what time the astronaut is to be dropped off at his hotel. We calculate how many more figure eights we will need to do, and the number is alarming. We stare at the clipping of Jean once more. We wonder where she is right now. We wonder if there are new ways of kissing that, without us, she is now learning.

6

The Astronaut of the Year wakes up violently, shouting random crazy things. He then yawns and rubs his eyes like a baby and says, "If I am not sitting beside a young woman in ten seconds, I am going to murder you, you coward." We have had enough. We pull over as quickly as we can in front of a bar with a picture of two big peaches, side by side, lit up on a white sign. On the sign, the peaches are dripping wet with cartoon water. The bar is called Hotsies. It is a bar we know well. Inside, the lovely waitresses who serve fried chicken wings wear hot orange shorts and white T-shirts that are constantly being soaked with water. They are in a perpetual wet T-shirt contest, and the customers pick the winners by giving lavish tips, which are counted at the end of their shifts. The winner is given all the other girls' tips, which is unfair but works in the customers' favor, because the waitresses have to be very, very friendly. We park and go around to help the astronaut out of the car, but he pushes our hands away. He tells us we are the most useless human he has ever met. Because we are as pitiful as we are, we are happy to have made some kind, any kind of impression on him. At a table inside the fake-cigarette-and-sawdust-aroma bar, the astronaut announces he wants a drink. He pounds the table. He whistles at the girls—girls who are not even as old as his dentures. We feel embarrassed for him. He notices. He digs into the pocket of his silver military space outfit. He takes out a shiny silver quarter and holds it up. "This has been to space," the astronaut says, holding the quarter under our nose. "This is the only thing at the table besides me that even counts." At that moment we decide that maybe there is a reason the Astronaut of the Year is so lonely. We do our best to ignore him. We secretly unfold the clipping of Jean and place it in our lap to help maintain our nonphysical, nonviolent, self-affirming composure. We watch in horror as the Astronaut of the Year grabs the clipping of Jean, stares at it, regards our face, and asks, "Did she leave you?"

We say, "Yes, very recently."

The astronaut says, "In the vast configuration of things, one man's heartbreak doesn't amount to a hill of beans. I know. I've been up there. I've seen what's important and what isn't. One man and one woman don't count for much." We ask for the clipping back, and he obliges, mocking and sneering. We fold it back up and apologize to ourselves and to the paper Jean for being so spineless, so small, so weak.

5

The Astronaut of the Year always has to have a countdown before he does anything, we discover ungratefully. Before he takes a sip of the lime gimlet he has ordered, he shouts, "Ten, nine, eight, seven, six, five, four, three, two, one!" and takes a gulp that drains the green glass in an instant. He spots a lovely tall waitress in a see-through white top, slick and playful as a cartoon seal, and waves her over. As she struts, pouting her lips, he counts down her approach: "Ten, nine, eight, seven, six, five, four, three, two, one." At the end of an hour in the bar, when the Astronaut of the Year is very drunk, befuddled, and as sad as a painting of an old silver clown, he lowers his head and counts, "Ten, nine, eight, seven, six, five, four, three, two, one," before he begins crying. We decide the hotel is the best place for him now and try to lead him to the car. He is stiff in our arms. He is like a statue of himself, but mysteriously weeping. We walk him outside, and he begins humming the national anthem. He salutes a torn red, white, and blue awning, which he confuses for a flag, before blacking out in the backseat.

4

The Astronaut of the Year wakes up again very quickly and says he is sorry. He says he is very hungry and only acting out. He says he promises he will act like an adult from now on. He says he will take us, "You and your paper girlfriend there," out to a lovely dinner. We are also hungry. We are very tired, and the inhibitor drugs may be wearing off. We are tempted by his sad, moonlit blue eyes into forgiveness. We accept his apology but decide on going to the most expensive restaurant we can find, which is a French place that even French people would accuse of being too trendy—all glass windows and small portions and waiters with tongues that never stop clucking. We are seated quickly, and I take out the clipping of Jean and give her her own seat. I can barely see her from where I am sitting, which is not very different from the real Jean.

3

The Astronaut of the Year forgets his promise and demands to wear his big space helmet in the fancy restaurant. He struggles to breathe inside it for a while and then sets it on the table like a magnificent fishbowl, his breath still foggy on the inside of the glass. He is ruining this anniversary dinner for us and knows it, but to him, nothing but his own happiness matters. We find it fitting that we are spending our anniversary with him, as this was exactly how we remember Jean always acting. We do not order coffee or dessert, because the astronaut has begun claiming neighboring tables in the name of the United States. He jabs a fork into a white circular table directly behind us, pushing past its occupants, and announces, "We have come so far. In the name of the United States, this moon we do righteously claim."

2

The Astronaut of the Year loses his vim after dinner, and we escort him back to his hotel. He demands that we see him up to his room. We oblige because we cannot lose this job. There were incidents at other jobs. There were perhaps several felonies. We escort the astronaut to his door. He demands that we tuck him in. We sigh without enough strength to actually sigh. We watch in horror as the astronaut undresses and puts on some other shiny silver space suit before climbing into bed. We wonder if it is actually a space suit or perhaps just fancy pajamas. We turn off the light and say good night. We begin to close the door when the Astronaut of the Year lets out a loud cry before bursting into an explosion of tears.

1

The Astronaut of the Year begs for us to turn on the light. We do. He wipes his eyes and says he has made many, many mistakes. He has chosen fame over love, glory over friendship, and fortune over family. He says at his age he has no one, no one, no one. We think of Jean making her television series and wonder if she feels the same way. We hope she feels the same way and then see how terrible it is, the feeling, and then change our mind, hoping she feels the same way but only for as long as we are feeling it. We sit on the edge of the bed. We hold the astronaut's hand. He is shaking like an epileptic. We think this man is about to die of loneliness. We think and think and think of how tomorrow, after all this, our customer service will probably still be negatively rated.

0

The Astronaut of the Year has calmed down after a glass of milk from room service. He sits up and says suddenly, "Up there, it doesn't hurt so bad. Here, it is like a ten-ton weight on my chest."

"What? Hurt? What hurts?" we ask, nervous it may be something medical.

"Up there, there's no gravity."

"Yes," we say. "So?" we say.

"So your heart isn't so durn heavy."

We nod because we don't know what else to say. We are young and arrogant and angry, and although we have driven the shuttle car thousands of miles, we have not been anywhere, really. We will never go to space. We will do all we can to avoid staring at the void any longer than necessary. We know we will never be anything more than what we were meant to be: average, human, infinitely predictable, infinitely imperfect. We know, even in our darkest moments, we will never be this lonely. We wait and wait until he falls asleep. We leave beside him, on his pillow, the paper clipping of Jean, lying like a miniature bride. We say good-bye to them both. We leave the lights on. We creep out slowly.

ABOUT THE AUTHOR

Joe Meno is the author of three novels, *Tender as Hellfire, How the Hula Girl Sings,* and *Hairstyles of the Damned,* which has been translated into German, Russian, and Italian. A contributing editor to *Punk Planet* and winner of the Nelson Algren award for short fiction, Meno lives in Chicago, where he teaches creative writing at Columbia College Chicago.